THE DAY BEFORE
YESTERDAY

The Day Before Yesterday

HISTORICAL ESSAYS
ON THE LIVING PAST

Donald Gregory

Donald Gregy

Christmas 2003

ISBN: 0-86381-371-4

*Cover illustration: Anne Lloyd Morris
Cover design: Alan Jones*

*First published in 1997 by Gwasg Carreg Gwalch,
12 Iard yr Orsaf, Llanrwst, Conwy, Wales. LL26 0EH.
☎ (01492) 642031*

Printed and Published in Wales.

*The photographs of Pennant Melangell church, which appear on page 136
and on the back-cover are reproduced by courtesy of Mick Sharp, Caernarfon.*

. . . to Helen, who has travelled the road with me.

*'The future never lies ahead of us,
but always comes flying over our heads from behind.'*
Confucius

Contents

Foreword

This book has been written for enthusiastic, non-academic readers in the hope that their enjoyment in studying the past may be further enhanced. An attempt has here been made, in dealing separately with a number of widely-differing topics, to show, for example, the importance of such basic essentials as salt and water, to assess the part played in world history by epidemics of diseases like bubonic plague, to explain in simple terms, enclosures, guilds, banking and tollgates, to unravel the mysteries of ostracism, and above all to relate historical events to everyday life. Thirty years ago and more Jessie, who cleaned for us, having the previous night watched on television a dramatic reconstruction of a famous historical event, talked enthusiastically about it the next morning when she came to work. She was an original, quite uneducated but with an enquiring mind and she wanted an answer to her question. 'Was it true?' she wanted to know, referring to the TV programme, or 'Was it just History?'

A typical early medieval scratch dial,
to be found on the south wall of the church.

Marking Time

Homo Sapiens in his slow and often painful struggle towards a civilised state has occasionally made valuable advances, one of which occurred when he discovered the usefulness of organising and categorising his knowledge and experiences. As this process developed it became desirable to know at what stage in the past certain important contributions to the store of knowledge had taken place. In most early societies stories of outstanding happenings or myths were handed down, usually by word of mouth from one generation to another, so that social traditions came into being. Such happenings, true or distorted, often provided historical starting points for a culture to which later events could be related. Important examples of such starting points were the celebration in Greece of the first Olympic Games and in Rome of the foundation of that city. Seeing that so much of Western European history has stemmed from the histories of

Greece and Rome, it is not really surprising that the earliest systems of marking time in the west were based on the first Olympic Games and the Foundation of Rome, both events taking place, according to tradition, within twenty years of each other in what we should call the eighth century BC.

The city states of ancient Greece, separate political entities as they were, and frequently warring with each other, yet came together every four years for the celebration of the Olympic Games, which were athletic, intellectual and aesthetic, a modern Olympic Games and an *Eisteddfod* rolled into one. The earliest such festival took place at the summer solstice in 776 BC at Olympia, in the Peloponnese of Greece. Greeks called the four years that elapsed between one games and the next an olympiad and gradually the practice grew of counting the passing of time in multiples of four years. The tendency was systematised by a Sicilian historian, Timaeus, who lived in Athens (352-256 BC). Thereafter the whole of Greek history was recorded in terms of the number of olympiads that had elapsed since 776 BC. Thus Pericles whose death, according to our method of counting the years, occurred in 429 BC, died in the eighty-seventh olympiad.

In Rome, a most unreliable tradition insisted that the city had been founded in 753 BC, which in time came to be accepted as the starting point for a Roman chronology. Hence, Carthage, which was destroyed by the Romans in 146 BC, was, according to this chronology, sacked in 607 AUC (AB URBE CONDITA, which meant 'from the foundation of the city'.)

The coming of Christianity eventually caused both these early chronologies to be superseded by providing a unifying system. This separation of the chronicling of human events into two sections, those that took place before the birth of Christ and those that occurred after, did not come about until the sixth century AD, when the change was suggested by Dionysius Exiguus, a scholar, monk and theologian, who lived in Rome. The Christian church accepted this most meaningful division in the history of mankind, though it should be pointed out that Dionysius put the vital division between the two eras between three and six years too late.

Christ was certainly born BC, in all probability, in 4 BC!

Some consideration must now be given to the very difficult question of how early Europeans, like the Romans, actually devised their calendars. In an agricultural society there had to be a very close relationship between the seasons and the calendar, but for this to come about, society needed the services of astronomers, whose functions in Rome were usurped by priests, who rarely knew much astronomy. In addition, the first Roman calendar was related to the lunar year which, of course, has thirteen months. It is not perhaps surprising that despite the occasional adding of an extra month to the dawdling calendar, the gap between the calendar and the seasons grew ever wider. By the middle of the first century BC (that is to say, by about 700 AUC), the position had become so bad that the calendar was more than three months wrong by the sun. Julius Caesar, having made himself master of Rome, though faced by many a daunting political problem, was wise enough to pay serious attention to the crying need for some reform of the calendar. The seat of astronomical knowledge was Alexandria, to which city Caesar had recourse. He listened to the advice of the foremost astronomer of the day, Sosigenes. Back in Rome, Caesar applied the wisdom of Sosigenes, incorporating it in the Julian Calendar, which, unlike its predecessor, was based on the solar year, which consisted of three hundred and sixty five and a quarter days. From then on the year would consist of three hundred and sixty five days with every fourth year having an extra day. This new calendar was to serve Europe well until by the sixteenth century AD, astronomers recommended a change, though not of a fundamental nature. A gap was once again beginning to open up between the calendar and the seasons.

In 1582 Pope Gregory XIII substituted for the Julian Calendar what came to be called the Gregorian or New Style Calendar; by a papal edict the change was made in October 1582, when ten days were lost. The new calendar was at once accepted in Rome, Spain, Portugal and in parts of Italy. France adopted it six months later and in the following year the Roman Catholic states of Germany followed suit. It was not until 1700 that the Protestant states of

Germany, Denmark and Sweden agreed to adopt the new calendar. Protestant England held aloof until September 1752, by which time the gap between the calendar and the sun had widened to eleven days. The day after September 2nd 1752 became September 14th amid a public outcry of "Give us back our eleven days". The Julian Calendar continued to be used in pre-revolutionary Russia, as anything suggested by Rome was regarded as anathema in Moscow. The change to the Gregorian Calendar finally came to Moscow in December 1917, being one of the very first acts of the new revolutionary government of Lenin.

Many historians in the past, finding themselves confronted by a vast accumulation of recorded facts, have tended to put the past into compartments; but for doing this, it was believed, no manageable or coherent account of the past would have been possible. There is some truth in this view but its limitations should be observed. No-one will dispute the division of English history into Tudor and Stuart times, because, although there are better ways of studying what went on here between 1485 and 1714 than by a chronological outline, yet at least the Tudors did rule from 1485 to 1603 and the Stuarts did follow them from 1603 to 1714. It is, however, when consideration be given to such broad sweeps of the past as the Dark Ages and the Middle Ages, that a note of warning needs to be sounded. By the term "Middle Ages" in a European context, is generally implied the thousand years that elapsed between the fall of the Western Roman Empire in 476 and the capture by the Turks of the capital of the Eastern Roman Empire, Constantinople, in 1453; in English history the Middle Ages comprise no less than our history from the establishment of the Saxon Heptarchy in the fifth century until the accession of Henry VII after the victory at Bosworth in 1485. Again the so-called Dark Ages were thought to have descended upon Europe when the Roman Empire fell in the fifth century AD and to have ended rather mysteriously when they were merged into the Middle Ages somewhere about the year 1200. The temptation to proceed further with this matter has to be resisted; historians are such fierce individualists that a debate, say, on when did modern history begin could prove as lengthy as it would be unproductive. To sum up, periods and categories are valid enough, always provided that the writer and the reader share a common vigilance.

The tyranny of dates is over. Nevertheless, it is as well to remember why it was ever thought necessary to attach dates to events and to learn them. Dates are no less and no more than pegs on which to hang things. If something better than a peg is to hand, so much the better, but if no workable alternative is forthcoming, history would be little more than a meaningless jumble of past events. For example, it is of interest to some readers to be told that in one and the same year (that the year was 1775 is less important), a skirmish took place in America that was to prove to be the prelude to the War of Independence and in England on Broad Ha'penny Down, the Hambledon Cricket Club introduced the third stump!

Obviously a sense of time is better than a mechanical knowledge of dates. Some people, however, as they grow older, may forget that their ability to see, for instance, the Battle of Hastings in something like historical perspective is due very largely to the fact that there are convenient links in their minds between 1066 and the present. Magna Carta and the Battle of Bosworth, the Armada and the Civil War, the Act of Union and the Industrial Revolution all help to show that Hastings was one link in a chain of events. The problem that many adults have to face is the difficulty of grasping in the mind great tracts of time, the difficulty of building a strong bridge between the present and past. One possible answer to this challenge is provided by a scaling down of time to more manageable proportions.

A thousand years has but the vaguest meaning to many people, whereas one year has solid substance. The scale suggested is that one year of history should be reckoned as one hour. On this time-scale Britain became an island less than a year ago, Stonehenge is but six months old, Christ died three months ago and it is only five weeks since the Battle of Hastings; it is just over a month since John met the barons at Runnymede, while Drake drove the fireships into Calais Roads a mere fortnight ago. It is only a week since Waterloo was fought and the RAF won the Battle of Britain a day or two ago!

Should this approach seem unacceptable, there is another way that has stood up well to the test of experience. Think of a friend or a relative whose age is about 75, then try to achieve a time-sense based on the life of this septuagenarian and on successive lives of others of the same age. It may come as something of a shock to realise that it requires but five successive lives of seventy-five year olds to bridge the gap between Guy Fawkes' attempt to blow up Parliament and the present. Once this approach is accepted — and imaginatively grasped — the past will race towards the present. The Battle of Hastings was fought less than thirteen lifetimes ago, while only twenty-seven such lifetimes separate us from the Britain that was raided in 55 BC by Julius Caesar; his despatches, sent home from this reconnaisance, constituted, be it remembered, the first chapter in our written history.

Bryn Celli Ddu
Anglesey

Neolithic Britain

The slow progress of man from complete savage to sophisticated citizen has taken so long that without some rather artificial divisions, a coherent account of developments could hardly have been attempted. In these northern latitudes there were three or four ice ages, which were interspersed with interglacial periods; in the latest of these ice ages, which ended between 9 and 10,000 BC, some human life appeared, the rudimentary existence of these early men in caves becoming known as palaeolithic, or belonging to the old stone age. When the ice began to melt, the caves became dark and wet and no longer habitable, so their occupants were forced to leave them and to learn to adjust to the new conditions. This time of transition was known as mesolithic, or the middle stone age. By about 6000 BC enough of the ice had melted to raise the level of the sea and in consequence these mesolithic men found themselves living on an island, where some two thousand years later their descendants were joined by successful invaders from across the sea. These newcomers, who were slight of stature and dark in countenance, either came from the Iberian peninsula or crossed the channel after coming up the Rhone Valley. These people are called neolithic and they introduced the culture of the new stone age.

Their ancestors had lived in the Middle East, where between 6000 and 5000 BC great changes had taken place, especially in the three river valleys of the Nile, the Tigris and the Euphrates. These changes gave rise to a revolution in the way of living that had no equal in importance until the Industrial Revolution two hundred years ago. New farming methods were devised which were so successful that for the first time there was surplus food. This not only led to a rapid increase in population but also freed some men from the task of growing food, enabling them to become specialists in making the new tools which the farmers required. These craftsmen in turn needed raw materials to supply which a trading class came into existence. The new society that emerged from this first division of labour comprised farmers, craftsmen and traders. These new ideas slowly crossed Europe, partly because the increased population wanted somewhere to live, partly because the traders were searching for new sources of raw materials and partly because farmers, having exhausted their fields, were always on the lookout for new untilled lands. The further west these neolithic men advanced, the simpler were the changes they brought, until when they finally reached Britain, they brought with them only the basic knowledge of mixed farming and skills in simple crafts like weaving and pottery. In their flimsy cross-channel boats, however, were precious cargoes indeed; sheep, cattle, seeds of wheat, and looms.

These people were the first settlers in these islands; they were too the first people to make any impression on the landscape. The general pattern of life seems to have been that the men looked after the animals, while the women were responsible for growing food.

Neolithic farmers, having abandoned the nomadic habits of the previous inhabitants here, lived in communities and hence at death were all buried in the same place. The long barrow, which is the chief clue to a neolithic settlement, was in reality a cemetery with a roof on top; in the course of nearly two thousand years of neolithic settlement here there was, not surprisingly, considerable variation in the types of chambered tombs in favour and indeed in the shapes of the covering mounds, not all of which were long. Most chambered tombs however consisted of a number of burial compartments, linked by passages or galleries and roofed over with immense capstones. When such a barrow was deemed full, it was covered over with a large mound of earth. Such information as there is of these neolithic people is largely derived from the study of the grave goods that have been excavated, from which it is clear that the flint tools and weapons that they used were very skilfully made and far superior to the rough and ready implements of mesolithic and palaeolithic men. These barrows have also revealed polished stone axes of a high quality and a good deal of pottery of varying types.

Most of the neolithic barrows that have survived are in the coastal areas in the west and north-west of the British Isles and in the off-shore islands; the Orkneys, the Shetlands, the Isles of Scilly and Anglesey are particularly rich in such remains. Later Neolithic settlers, who crossed the channel, went up the river-valleys of the south-west or ventured into habitable hilly country. Their long barrows have been classified as belonging to the Severn-Cotswold type. Of the many neolithic barrows recognisable as such, six have been chosen here for special mention, partly because they represent the two different invasions, partly because they are much more accessible to the visitor today than are most barrows, and partly because each group of three can be seen in a single day.

The first group of megalithic tombs is in the north-west of Wales, in Gwynedd and in Anglesey. The barrow at Capel Garmon lies hidden half a mile south of the village of the same name, which is itself accessible by steep country roads both from Llanrwst, which is twelve miles south of Conwy on the A470, and from

Betws-y-coed, on the A5. Prudence suggests leaving the car in the village and going on foot to the barrow, which enjoys a quite magnificent situation above the Conwy Valley. Nearby is a farm where essential Department of the Environment literature may be obtained.

The ninety feet long barrow, which was excavated sixty years ago, is similar in appearance to the Severn Cotswold type, to be visited in the second group; it possesses a horned forecourt which leads to a false entrance. The true entrance, which is from the south side, gives access along a passage to a central area on both sides of which were burial chambers. Pottery found in the barrow belonged both to neolithic and to later times, indicating that burials took place there both in later neolithic and in Bronze Age times.

The other barrows in this group are both in Anglesey and were associated with a neolithic culture pattern that was widespread across the Irish Sea. Indeed Irish-type megalithic monuments like these two in Anglesey can also be found in the Hebrides and even as far north as in the Orkneys, where there is a particularly fine specimen at Maes Howe, north-east of Stromness.

To get to Bryn Celli Ddu, leave the A5 on Anglesey at Llanfair Pwllgwyngyll, taking the lefthand turning A4080; a mile or so along this road turn right on to a minor road, finger-posted to Llanddaniel-fab. Before this village is reached a marker post on the righthand side indicates that Bryn Celli Ddu lies in a field to the south of a long straight farm lane (barred to cars). This barrow is visually the most impressive in Wales because it has been partially restored. The Department of the Environment booklet, obtainable at the farm, is absolutely essential, if one is to understand the intricacies of the place. Today's mound covers only a small part of the original cemetery but gives a rare sense of entering into another world. A torch is recommended in order to appreciate the interior where of particular interest is a central pillar stone. Another stone (a replica of the original) in a pit outside the chamber, reveals an incised pattern which proves its relationship to the Irish tombs and to Barclodiad-y-Gawres, next to be visited.

In order to enter this second barrow in Anglesey, which is in the

18

north-west corner of the island, it is necessary first to go east to Beaumaris Castle, to obtain the key for which a deposit has to be paid. Barclodiad-y-Gawres is situated two miles south of the seaside resort of Rhosneigr and dominates the Bay of Trecastell, where a car may be left, before the climb is made along the cliff to the barrow; the roof of the barrow has been replaced by a concrete dome, which was considered necessary to protect the tomb from the ravages of time and vandals. With the aid of a torch the passage which is twenty feet long will be seen to lead to a central area, off which there is a single chamber to the east and a double one to the west. What makes this barrow so important, however, is the decoration which adorns five of the stones there. Their spirals and chevrons provide another close link with the great neolithic tombs of Ireland, strengthening the proof that the men who carved these stones came from the Iberian peninsula, where such carvings abound.

The three long barrows in the second group that can be visited in a single day all belong to the Severn-Cotswold type. The first bears the mysterious name of Wayland's Smithy, a name that has been attached to it for only the last thousand years and therefore has no connection with the New Stone Age. Wayland, according to tradition, was a blacksmith who was prepared to shoe a traveller's horse, should the need arise; a suitable coin left on one of the stones would be enough to secure a well-shod horse for the traveller on the following morning! This barrow lies in an area associated with horse myths; nearby is the Vale of the White Horse, whose most prominent feature is the White Horse of Uffington, which probably dates from early Iron Age times. Wayland Smithy, which is quite close to the splendid White Horse, is six miles west of Wantage, just under the Ridgeway in a sheltered clump of beech trees. (There is a convenient place in which to park a car half a mile away). When excavated in the 1960s, an earlier burial place was discovered underneath the long barrow; here were found the remains of fourteen bodies. The long barrow itself, which is dated to about 3500 BC, is a passage grave with a pair of burial chambers each side, originally roofed with heavy slabs of stone before being covered with a grassed mound of chalk. Before erosion and excavation, the mound was about two hundred feet long and fifty feet wide.

Next, to Gloucestershire, to see Hetty Pegler's Tump, which is three miles south-west of Stroud. The barrow, named after the wife of the seventeenth century owner of the field in which it stands, is quite near to the road and clearly marked, but the key has to be obtained from a house half a mile down the road. Once again a torch is essential. Unfortunately there was insufficient excavation here in the early nineteenth, as well as vandalism in the twentieth century, with the result that much of value has been lost. However, despite the ruined chambers which have had to be blocked up, it is a memorable experience to penetrate the twenty-two feet long subterranean passage which is only five feet high; it gives access to two burial chambers on the left side and another one at the end of the passage, while the lost chambers were originally on the righthand side. To quote Jacquetta Hawkes, from her *A Guide to the Prehistoric and Roman Monuments in England and Wales* . . . "Here at last it is possible to have the sensation of being closed in a tomb and in the earth; it is dark and although the chambers are not large, the megalithic architecture gives an impression of massive grandeur."

For the finale of this summer day's excursion, a pleasant country walk is involved. Belas Knap, meaning Beacon Mound, is further north in Gloucestershire, six miles north of Cheltenham. A marker post stands two miles along the minor road that runs from Winchcombe to Charlton Abbots. The long barrow, which stands out on the skyline a thousant feet up, has suffered even more than most sites from premature excavation as well as from vandalism. However, today's visitors have good reason to be very grateful to those patient archaeologists who in the late nineteen twenties and early thirties carried out a highly skilful and most rewarding restoration so that up there in the windswept Cotswolds it is now possible to get a very clear picture of what a long barrow must have looked like when first it was sealed more than four thousand years ago. The mound is about one hundred and seventy feet long and sixty feet wide; at its widest part there is a horned forecourt which leads to an impressive false entrance, while the three burial chambers from which thirty skeletons were recovered, are to be found in the sides of the green mound.

No account of neolithic times in Britain can be considered complete without at least a passing reference to Stonehenge, which is probably the most famous prehistoric site in Europe. Certainly the first stones were erected there in neolitic times, probably soon after 3000 BC; equally certainly, most of the building took place hundreds of years later in the transitional period that covered the overlapping of later neolithic and early Bronze Age times. The Druids have so often been associated with Stonehenge that it needs to be stressed that this priestly caste belonged to the Iron Age which flourished some two thousand years after the building of Stonehenge. The role played by Stonehenge in prehistoric times is still largely a matter of guesswork, beyond the obvious inference that it was a central meeting place.

This scene, depicting monks giving piggy-backs to nuns, illustrates the reversal of normal roles at Christmas.

Rituals of Rebellion

Even in our highly sophisticated social life of today we are, if we are young enough, occasionally allowed to let our hair down. Such occasions are April Fools' Day and, in some parts of the country, Mischief Night, which is neatly sandwiched between All Hallows E'en and Guy Fawkes Day. Early in April and again early in November each year strange things are allowed to happen, though it is far from clear why society gives its consent to such unusual licence.

A similar state of affairs, though more ritualistically organised, took place in simple societies until fairly recently. In such societies a feature of life at certain critical seasons of the year was the indulgence in ritualistic practices which had the appearance of mutiny in the same way that handing the teacher a brick, wrapped in gift paper, on the first of April might appear mutinous. At the Spring sowing and in the Autumn harvest seemingly mutinous ceremonies took place, referred to as rituals of rebellion by social anthropologists, which had the avowed purpose of relieving social tension. Social anthropologists believe that these institutionalised protests, openly expressing social tension, helped to increase rather than to weaken the unity of the social system. For instance, in partriarchal societies in southern Africa, women, who normally had an absolutely inferior role in the social order of things, were encouraged at these times of social tension to behave with the utmost immodesty; they had to wear men's clothes and they had to do things that were normally absolutely quite tabu for women to do, such as herding and milking cattle. In addition custom prescribed that they should strut about naked and sing lewd songs, while the men and boys were required by the same social compulsion to run away and hide, as women would normally do in such circumstances; such a reversal of normal social roles was thought to increase the prospects for a good harvest. These ceremonies in Zululand were banned by the South African government in the 1930s and it is interesting to note that thereafter whenever a crop failed the Zulu farmers blamed their government for banning these rituals of rebellion.

In the ancient world of Roman times the reversal of social roles was obligatory during the Saturnalia, which overlapped the celebration of the winter solstice. Joseph Strutt, in his *Sports and Pastimes of the People of England*, writing in 1801, said "Whimsical transpositions of dignity are derived from the ancient Saturnalia, when the masters waited upon their servants, who were honoured with mock titles and permitted to assume the state and deportment of their lords." Amid all the customs of the Saturnalia, which dealt with specific ways and means of best enjoying the pleasures of the flesh, were certain clear requirements to change the normal order of social life. Along with the election of a Lord of Misrule, who was to be in charge of festivities, were fixed rules, which ensured equality of eating and drinking. One such stated: 'When the rich man shall feast his slaves, let his friends serve with him.' Again another law, laid down for the proper observance of the Roman Saturnalia, demanded thus: "All men shall be equal, slave and free, rich and poor, one with another." All that was to happen in a world where the social order was based on slavery. In the Roman New Year, when the festivities still went on, other strange reversals of social roles took place, anticipating in some ways the later customs already referred to in Zululand. In these new year ceremonies men dressed up as women and women as men and in addition men sometimes wore animal skins and animal masks. This latter practice seems to have had a very early origin indeed; for in caves in the Dordogne homo sapiens as early as 30,000 B.C. had painted on the walls men disguised as animals.

These were some of the traditions inherited by a Europe, which had become Christianised; this was part of the frequently recurring problem of the medieval church, which had either to reject out of hand all surviving pagan practices and risk making no more Christian converts or somehow to produce a synthesis of pagan practices and Christian ideas, which would aim to win over traditionalists without giving irreparable offence to Christian purists. At first the Church took a stand and forbade time-honoured practices but eventually Christian leaders very sensibly tried with varying degrees of success to adapt these older customs to Christian uses; gradually the worst excesses were overcome, although well into Tudor times the Lord of Misrule continued to enjoy his annual exercise of power. On the continent and more especially in France, strange pseudo-religious practices, involving the reversal of social roles, resisted for many years all attempts to suppress them. During the twelve days of Christmas a bishop of fools was elected, who then led into the local cathedral a procession of attendants, clad in the costumes of pantomime; this retinue as it processed sang indecent songs. These farcical scenes, which frequently broke every canon of good taste, usually ended with the bishop blessing the congregation.

Similar practices in England were brought to an end earlier; they certainly did not survive the fourteenth century in any extreme form. They were eventually whittled down to the annual election, often on the sixth of December, St Nicholas' Day, of a boy bishop, who, suitably attired, was required to lead the procession of clergy in the cathedral, where he had to preach a sermon to which the cathedral dignitaries had to appear to listen with a show of respect. The service invariably ended with the Dean kneeling to receive a blessing from the Boy Bishop, an interesting illustration of the attempt by the church authorities to canalise the desire to reverse social roles. The election of boy bishops died out in the middle of the sixteenth century but it had by that time become little more than a pleasant and harmless piece of pageantry.

Today rituals of rebellion are rare indeed; one such is the brief reversing of roles at Christmas, when in many units of the Army the officers still wait on the men at dinner. This particular ritual, be it noted, would not be possible in a badly-disciplined army. Again, on Boxing Day, when traditionally the pantomime season opens, men still dress up as women and women as men, but politically today such rituals are non-existent. The political systems of civilised man are so insecurely founded that, if rituals of rebellion were encouraged, these systems, so far from being strengthened, would probably be swept away altogether. A Lord of Misrule today might well exceed his prescribed term of office.

In Athens opposite the two famous hills, the Areopagus and the Acropolis was a third, the Pnyx, where the Assembly met in the open air. All citizens had a right to vote and once a year if the majority voted for anyone to be exiled, they could bring it about by writing his name on a broken piece of pottery (an ostrakon).

Ostracism

Every society at one time or another has to face up to the problem of deciding what to do with those of its members whose attitudes or actions are thought to constitute a threat to the well-being of the security of the rest. In Anglo-Saxon England, for instance, such a man became an outlaw; he was thereafter liable to be killed at sight by anyone who recognised him, his lands and worldly goods forfeit to the crown. Again, in Roman times, the punishment for the rejected citizen was exile; the banished Roman not only lost his property but also his status as a citizen, his exile, which was for an indefinite period, invariably being for life.

This chapter will deal with another way of solving this particular problem, which was practised in Athens for just under a century, from the end of the sixth century BC to nearly the end of the fifth century; it was an experiment which was doubly interesting because it coincided with the great days of Athenian democracy and concerned some of its outstanding leaders.

Shortly after 510 BC, after a disturbed period of autocratic government in Athens, Cleisthenes set himself up as the champion of the people and was entrusted by them with the task of reforming the constitution. That Athens in the next century was able to acquire a democratic form of government was very largely due to these reforms of Cleisthenes who, however, foresaw that the security and welfare of the state might occasionally be endangered either by the excessive ambition of one man or by the deadlock that might arise if two powerful leaders were in constant opposition to each other. Hence Cleisthenes ordained that the Assembly of the people should once a year be consulted to see if it considered that Athens would benefit from the banishment of any one citizen. If the Assembly favoured this course of action, a special meeting was then summoned at which the members, without debate or indeed without the naming of names, could, if they so desired, write on a broken piece of pottery (for which the Greek word was 'ostrakon') the name of the man whose continued presence in the city was thought a public danger. Should a majority of potsherds bear the same name, he was at once ostracised. The victim of this legal process was thereupon required to leave Athens at once and live elsewhere for the following ten years but he lost neither property nor civil rights. He could return if he wished after the ten years of banishment and serve his city again. Sometimes the service that he rendered after his return was distinguished indeed and to the great benefit of the city he had once been forced to leave.

Readers will be left to judge for themselves as to the merits or demerits of a system which twice in ten years could deprive Athens of such distinguished statesmen as Aristeides and Themistocles, both of whose names would figure prominently on any honours board of history in Athens of the fifth century BC. The first half of this century was a severe testing time for the city states of Greece; the rising power of Persia was menacing from the east. Relentlessly her borders were being pushed further to the west until 490 BC the first Persian invasion of Greece took place, the avowed enemy being the city of Athens. The expedition, six hundred ships strong, crossed the Aegean Sea with an army of infantry and cavalry on board. In September the Persian fleet was beached at Marathon, the army disembarked and made ready for battle. A much smaller Athenian army marched the twenty-six miles from Athens to deal with this most alarming of emergencies, but against all the odds won the day. One of the army leaders on that glorious day of triumph was Aristeides. The first Persian attempt to lord it over Greece had failed, as her ships escaped back over the seas with the remnant of the defeated army. As a result of Marathon, Athens came to be regarded for the first time as the champion of the Greeks, who thereafter increasingly looked to her for leadership and protection.

Aristeides was rewarded for his services by being elected archon for the following year (archons or rulers were elected annually). That there would be a second Persian invasion was taken for granted so that the main task for the leaders of Athens was to prepare for the next challenge, which in fact was forthcoming ten years later in 480 BC. Before that second and infinitely more terrible threat developed, Aristeides had had to leave the city. As vital decisions were being taken, the views of the two leading men, Aristeides and Themistocles, clashed; the policies of Themistocles on this occasion carried the day and the Assembly banished Aristeides from Athens.

The Persian army marched into Greece and after winning the Battle of Thermopylae, poured into the plain towards Athens, whose inhabitants evacuated the city and fled to the neighbouring islands. The issue was decided in a sea-battle at Salamis in the Saronic Gulf in September 480 BC. The greatly outnumbered Athenian fleet, led by Themistocles, gained a remarkable victory to which, be it noted, the ostracised Aristeides made his contribution. In the small island to which he had fled, he had succeeded in raising a few ships and the men to sail them. As his reward he was recalled to Athens where the very next year he was put in charge of the army which was in a state of readiness for dealing with the still undefeated Persian army. In 479 Aristeides led out his army and defeated the Persians at Plataea. The second Persian invasion was in disarray.

Twice in ten years Greece had been invaded; clearly much better defensive plans were required if the expected third invasion was to be frustrated. Hence the various city states of Greece, under the acknowledged leadership of Athens, formed themselves into a naval defensive alliance to deal with all future emergencies. The architect of this Confederacy of Delos was Aristeides. All participant states agreed to contribute men and ships or money to the common cause; one and all accepted without a second thought the assessments for the various contributions which Aristeides made. By this time he was generally known as Aristeides the Just; all men trusted him as a man of honour and absolute integrity. He died in 468 BC and left so little money that the state had to pay for his funeral.

The other great Athenian leader at the time of the Persian Wars to suffer ostracism was none other than Themistocles; born in 514 BC, even as a young man he proclaimed himself to be an intellectual with very strong political ambitions. Unlike his rival and contemporary, Aristeides, he shifted his ground very frequently as whim and self-interest dictated. He was a man of outstanding ability but of low moral standards; he was unscrupulous and corrupt but yet did far more than any other Athenian or indeed Greek to dispel the Persian nightmare.

In the breathing space afforded by the failure of the first Persian invasion at Marathon, Themistocles set himself the task of persuading his fellow citizens that the very survival of Athens would in the long run depend entirely on the possession of a large and well-trained navy. The methods he employed in bringing this fleet into being may sometimes have been suspect but his reasoning was always sound. The fortunate discovery in the 480s of a very rich vein of the purest silver in the state-owned silver mine at Laureion, on the coast north of Sunium, gave Themistocles just the opportunity he was looking for. Despite a great deal of opposition, he managed eventually to get the necessary permission to devote the windfall to the speedy enlargement of the Athenian fleet. It was during this vital debate, though the actual circumstances are not now clear, that the clash between him and Aristeides came to a head, which resulted in the latter's ostracism.

In 481 BC, his rival now withdrawn from the scene, Themistocles was elected chief archon and in the following year, when the Persian King Xerxes invaded Greece, Themistocles was made commander-in-chief of the fleet, which his statesmanship had brought about. As the Persian army marched inexorably south after its victory at Thermopylae, Themistocles saw his chance and managed to interpret the verdict of the oracle at Delphi, which he had been authorised to consult, in such a way that he was able to overcome the natural reluctance of many Athenians to leave their homes in the city and take refuge in the islands. The evacuation was sorrowfully carried out and before long the Persian army systematically destroyed the city but Themistocles had had the foresight to realise that the Persian army could not stay in Greece for very long, if the Persian navy should prove unable to keep the supply-lines open. To Themistocles the outcome of the war depended on the control of the sea, which he brilliantly gained by his superb strategy at the naval Battle of Salamis. The credit for this decisive victory belonged to him alone; on that September day in 480 BC his reputation was at its peak, his hold on Athenian affections seemingly unassailable. Before long the populace of Athens flocked back home where they set about rebuilding their homes in the ruined city. Themistocles, his thoughts still dwelling on the need to retain control of the sea, pleaded in vain that the new city should be built at the Peiraeus, but at least he did succeed in having long walls built to link the Peiraeus with the city of Athens, nearly five miles distant.

The preeminence of Themistocles in Athenian counsels was not to last, however; as has already been seen, Aristeides was recalled after his service to his city at Salamis. His record of integrity and unselfish service over the years seems to have contrasted favourably with the more mercurial but less reliable activities of Themistocles. The pendulum swung again; in the second clash between Aristeides and Themistocles, it was Themistocles who was ostracised. In 472 he retired to Argos, in the Peloponnese; from there he went to Asia Minor, where in 449 BC he died in office as the governor of a Persian province! It is indeed ironical that the man whose far-sightedness had done so much to save Greece from Persian conquest, should play no part in organising Greece into the Confederacy of Delos, whose initial task was to stave off any future Persian attack.

There were, of course, other occasions in the fifth century BC, when the ostracism of leading men in Athens took place, notably that of Cimon in 461 BC, but, as the century wore on, and the Confederacy of Delos developed into an Athenian Empire, political groups grew ever more divisive; ostracism in those circumstances became more and more a weapon to be wielded in the war of party politics. A political device, which had been set in motion in a high-minded endeavour to safeguard a democratic way of doing things, had deteriorated to such an extent that, when it was last taken advantage of in 417 BC, public opinion turned against it and it was used no more. By this time too the days of Athenian democracy itself were ominously numbered.

The well at Llangennith, Gower

Wells

In this chapter attention will be focused on those underground supplies of water without which life in early times could not have been maintained, and near which early settlements had to be sited because of the difficulty of storing water and the unavailability of suitable containers for its transport. It is therefore hardly surprising that many wells may have been found near prehistoric sites, the findings of water-diviners frequently providing invaluable confirmation of this fact.

In Wales, very many early Christian meeting places were on Bronze Age sites as were many of their early burial grounds, circular churchyards, which are far from rare in the country, giving the clue to such continuity of usage. Very often in early days in Wales the Christian message was carried by missionaries who, in the hope of making religious conversions in promising localities, built for themselves simple dwellings which had of necessity to be put up near wells. If such simple huts were built, as they often were, on sites previously used by people of the Bronze Age, then the nearby wells will also have been utilised by the missionaries.

In addition, the authorities in the early Church encouraged the continued use of earlier and pagan religious sites, as the famous letter which Pope Gregory 1st sent to the abbot, Mellitus here in Britain attests. Mellitus had been sent here from Rome a few years after Augustine's original mission, to follow up its impact and to bring encouragement to Augustine. According to Bede, the Pope in AD 601 wrote: "When Almighty God shall bring you to the most reverend Bishop Augustine, tell him what I have determined upon, viz. that the temples of the idols in that nation ought not to be destroyed, but let the idols that are in them be destroyed . . . let altars be erected and relics be placed . . . for if these temples are well-built, it is requisite that they be converted from the worship of devils to the service of the true God . . . " In the event, not only were the instructions of the Pope obeyed and the buildings saved, but also in many instances the wells on which the pagan temples depended were also taken over, being blessed and often made sacred to the Virgin Mary. Many a well had a long and useful history before becoming holy.

Pagan wells, once blessed into holiness by Christian priests, were used to provide water for the purification of what had been pagan temples; thereafter the holy wells acted as suppliers of holy water for the fonts of those churches that often shared the same dedication as the wells. It was no uncommon occurrence for priests to bless prehistoric megaliths as well as wells, especially if they were in the vicinity of churches. Francis Jones, the acknowledged authority on the subject in Wales, cites in all over a hundred pagan sites in Wales which were converted to Christian use by the rededication of wells and megaliths or by the erection of new churches near recently sanctified wells.

Energetic readers may be interested to know that there are seven churchyards in Wales, where either a well may still be seen or where evidence of a well in former days is available. Enthusiasts in the historical wonderland of south-west Pembrokeshire are advised to go inland from St Davids (*Tyddewi*) to the village of Llandeloy (*Llan-lwy*) (GR 857267) where in the long village street stands a church, dedicated to St Teilo, which was most skilfully restored early in the twentieth century. If a summer visit is planned, only the general area between the church and the site of the well will be seen, so luxuriant and therefore forbidding is the surrounding bed of high nettles! Further east, in the Gower Peninsula, is Oxwich, whose church lies away from the village on a headland (GR 505862). On the landward side of the church, up an upward sloping bank under a yew tree will, with some difficulty, if the weather is dry, be found a well. The third area in Wales, where there was once a well in a churchyard is in Flintshire, south-east of Holywell (*Treffynnon*), near the modern church at Halkyn (*Helygain*). The well still exists but the church it one time served is no longer there, although the site is marked by a flat platform, around which are may yews, under which are a great many grave stones. Nearby is the well, whose GR is 209712. This former churchyard is quite near today's church; it is just across the road and over a wall!

The other four wells are easily found. Moving from north to south our first stop is in Anglesey at Cerrig Ceinwen, (GR 424738), three miles from Llangefni. The church nestles in the bottom of a dell, some fifteen feet below the level of the approach road, from which the path to the church through the churchyard leads past the well on the south side of the church. Until a few years ago this well satisfied all the needs of the village as well as supplying the font with christening water for many a century. On next to the Conwy Valley to one of the most remote churches in the whole of Wales, at Llangelynnin (GR 752737), about a mile north of Ro-wen. The church and churchyard are about nine hundred feet above the valley; the well is excellently preserved and is walled around except for a narrow entrance. Its water was renowned for curing the diseases of children. Next of these remarkable survivals is to be found ten miles west of Welshpool (*Y Trallwng*) in Powys at Llanfair Caereinion, whose church is on a hilly site in the middle of the town above the river Banwy. On the north side of the churchyard a stone path leads down to a well, (GR 104064), which was probably in use long before Christianity came to Wales. The last of the seven wells is to be seen, also in Powys, but much further south. Early in the fifteenth century during Owain Glyndŵr's revolt or war of independence, according to personal opinion, a battle was fought at Pilleth (GR 257693) on the hill above the church in whose churchyard is a well, dedicated to St Mary, whose water was thought able to cure eye diseases. In June 1402, a hot day in summer, the thirsty soldiers, engaged in the fighting, are said to have slaked their thirsts in this old well.

There is no area in the British Isles where the links between prehistory and the early Christian church are stronger than in the south-west corner of Pembrokeshire, where St David was born. It may even be that David chose this part of Wales for his mission because of the pagan challenge that the district afforded. At any rate a mile or so outside the city on a headland, overlooking St Bride's Bay, is to be found St Non's Chapel, dedicated to the mother of David, who is credited by tradition to have given birth to her illustrious son on this spot. In the meadow where this early shrine stands are still to be seen five standing stones, thought to be survivors of a stone circle erected there by men of the Bronze Age, who will have drawn their water from a well near St Non's Chapel, long since rededicated to the Virgin Mary. It is worth remembering that this well, which was probably the first of the Christian healing wells, had already been in widespread use for many centuries before the birth of David.

A few miles east of St Davids, along the south coast of Pembrokeshire, is the attractive village by the sea of Solva (*Solfach*); high up above it, a mile to the east, was once a thriving prehistoric settlement that in the course of time gave place to an equally thriving Christian settlement. Today all that remains is a farm whose name, St Elvis, perpetuates the dedication of a church which once stood nearby. This now vanished church was in existence at least as early as in the thirteenth century and had a rector as late as in 1884. The font survives and is now in use in the parish church down in Solva. Two cromlechs and the well that supplied the Bronze Age community were still visible sixty years ago, but alas all that now remains are the written accounts which mercifully are still available for scrutiny in the County Record Office in Haverfordwest.

In another part of Wales, further north in Powys, is the remote but substantial village of Llanfechain. Here there is no written record of early Christian missionaries, but there is a tantalising prospect. There is a church in a circular churchyard, a holy well 300 yards away and, in the churchyard, an unexcavated mound. All three, church, well and mound, are dedicated to the same saint — Garmon. The mound is called Twmpath Garmon and the well, Ffynnon Garmon. The likelihood is that there was a Bronze Age settlement where the church now stands, which was supplied by the well that is now in a farmyard, isolated in a sea of slurry! This pattern of circular churchyard, Bronze Age mound and holy well is repeated in many places in Wales.

In the middle ages, wells assumed great importance in the lives of most communities; in some places the well was second only to the parish church as a focal point in local society. It was a power-house to which people went to get cures for their ailments or to find out about the future or to have a spell put upon their enemies. There were healing wells and wishing wells and even cursing wells; such wells, while serving the community at all times in the year, were thought to be particularly potent at certain seasons, Palm Sunday, Easter Monday, Whit Sunday, Ascension Day and Trinity Sunday being especially favoured for visits and consultation.

Many of these wells still survive with local records to furnish the details of past practices. This is particularly true of Cornwall and Wales where wells were consecrated in great numbers as early Christianity spread. Of all the ancient wells of Wales none is more celebrated than the one associated with St Winifred at Holywell in Flintshire. The unfortunate Winifred, the legend insists, was decapitated by a thwarted would-be rapist, a spring appearing where her head touched the ground. The fact that Winifred was the niece of the seventh century missionary St Beuno ensured the fame of the story, especially as the holy man is credited with having successfully replaced his niece's head, enabling her to live for a further fifteen years, during which time she was to become the Abbess of Gwytherin, Conwy. (Those interested in her subsequent history are recommended to read Ellis Peters' historical thriller, *A Morbid Interest in Bones*). The healing qualities of St Winifred's well became so famous that a great cult developed there over the years. It is reported that among the many thousands of pilgrims to the spot were three kings of England, William I, Edward I and James II.

Very many wells retained into modern times their reputations for curing the sick, many of whom would have first to bathe in them and then where, as often happened in Wales, there was a prehistoric cromlech conveniently close, they would be carried there to lie in its shadow in the belief that a cure might thus be further hastened. Certainly a well in Glastonbury continued to enjoy well into the eighteenth century its reputation for performing miracles as, according to the local record, in the month of May 1751 no fewer than ten thousand people paid it a visit.

In the nineteenth century and in the early years of the twentieth century wells became popular as picnic sites; visitors who came to enjoy themselves, however, generally paid sufficient deference to ancient practice to continue to throw pins, preferable bent ones, into the wells, as their forebears had done. In central Wales a feature of these picnics was dancing and the drinking of sugared water. In one Cornish village where there was a well quite close to the parish church, the tradition had grown up that, after a wedding, matrimonial domination would pass to the man or woman who should first drink from the well after the ceremony. On one occasion it seems that the husband was thwarted in his ambition. According to tradition:

"I hastened as soon as the wedding was done,
    And left my wife in the porch,
    But in faith she had been wiser than me,
    For she took a bottle to church."

North of the border superstitious practices at wells were sternly frowned upon by the church authorities. In the seventeenth and eighteenth centuries instances were recorded of parishioners in Scotland being arraigned for going to the well on Sunday. The usual punishment meted out was a fine and the need to do penance for three successive Sundays in the church porch.

Every year on Ascension Day there is in parts of Derbyshire a kind of well festival; it is especially popular in the village of Tissington near Ashbourne, where this practice of well-dressing originated. Today the scene is extremely colourful with the various wells decked out with flowers and duly photographed by TV cameras. A church service is followed by ceremonies at the wells. In recent years, villages other than Tissington have also decorated their wells with flowers but the practice seems to have started early in the seventeenth century when, in a year of great and widespread drought, the wells of Tissington continued to flow, to the infinite relief of people in the neighbouring villages, who went there to collect the precious commodity when their own wells dried up. What started as a simple thanksgiving service has now passed into folklore and tradition.

In the last two hundred years wells have come into their own again for another reason; just as in the middle ages the sick went to wells to find cures for their ailments, so much more recently many people with certain disorders of the mind and body have, on the advice of their physicians, flocked to places like Bath and Matlock, Harrogate and Malvern, Buxton and Cheltenham and Llandrindod Wells to partake of the evil-smelling but health-giving sulphur and chalybeate springs. This modern rediscovery of the healing powers of wells seems to have begun in Belgium in the middle of the eighteenth century, when the small hill-top town of Spa became a fashionable resort, as its medicinal waters became known to the medical profession. Thus a new word was given to the English language and a new kind of holiday resort was made available to the chronically depressed and dyspeptic.

Hallstatt in the Alps, a cradle of Celtic culture, was founded because of the salt mines (still in production today) in the mountains behind the village.

Salt

Of all the commodities in everyday use none is more likely to be taken for granted than common salt; 'the stuff' it has been said 'that makes potatoes taste awful when you forget to put it in!' Everyday speech bears eloquent testimony to its great importance. In days when social distinctions were more rigorously maintained than they are today, it mattered a very great deal whether a guest was required to sit above or below the salt, which will have been contained in a large salt cellar, occupying a central position on the table. Even today, when we are being entertained, we tend to refer to eating someone's salt. Good people, we are assured, are the salt of the earth, while tall stories are generally received with a grain of salt. Spilling the salt as far back as in Roman times was regarded as an unlucky omen; in Leonardo da Vinci's painting of the Last Supper the salt cellar in front of Judas Iscariot has clearly been knocked over by his sleeve. Some of those who read this page may be slightly troubled if they spill any salt. They may even, if they are sure that no-one is looking their way, pick up a pinch of it with the fingers of the right hand, and throw it discreetly over their left shoulder! We also talk about trying to put some salt on the tail of our quarry. At one time too, at funerals, there was a custom of sprinkling salt inside the coffin; many people believed that the Devil, who was not supposed to exist but who illogically was thought to loiter in churchyards, disliked salt, presumably because it slowed down decomposition.

Yet the earliest people of whom the archaeological record informs us, had no knowledge of salt or apparently any need for it; early man in his nomadic state mostly lived on nuts and berries and, when he was in luck, on flesh which he will have eaten raw. Even in later times when he had learned how to use fire, his body will still have felt no need for salt because meat roasted on the open fire will have kept its mineral salts intact. There is a reference in the Odyssey to strange distant people who lived so far from the sea that Homer said that they had never even heard of it; indeed they ate their food without benefit of salt, a thing which no Greek would willingly have done. The need for salt may well have arisen when man dropped his nomadic habits and first settled down to become a rudimentary farmer; however simple the economy of these early social units may have been, the need for salt must in all probability have been felt because the crops they were then able to grow required salt in their cooking, as also did the meat, unless it was always roasted.

The Austrian city of Salzburg, celebrated today for the music festival held there to commemorate the birth of Mozart, has a much older claim to fame. As its name suggests, there is an abundance of salt in the area, which has been mined there continuously since prehistoric times. The famous Hallstatt culture of the early Iron Age was probably based on this region because of the local availability of salt. In addition to salt mines, there was a great number of brine springs in the neighbourhood from which salt was obtained by evaporation through allowing the salt-laden water to flow over heated pottery. Similar processes were being employed elsewhere in the Iron Age in Belgium and Brittany.

It is interesting to note that when men in these newly settled communities started to make offerings to their gods, they invariably included salt among the things they sacrificed. In this connection there is a significant reference in the Old Testament in Leviticus, chapter two, verse thirteen " . . . and every oblation of thy meat offering shalt thou season with salt. Neither shalt thou suffer the salt of the covenant of thy God to be lacking from thy meat offering; with all thine offerings thou shalt offer salt." A covenant of salt, mentioned here and elsewhere in the Old Testament, indicates an absolutely binding agreement, one that is as unchanging and as incorruptible as salt itself. In Numbers chapter eighteen, verse nineteen we read " . . . It is a covenant of salt for ever before the Lord unto thee and to thy seed with thee." And again, in the second Book of Chronicles, chapter thirteen, verse five " . . . Ought ye not to know that the Lord God of Israel gave the kingdom over Israel to David for ever, even to him and to his sons by a covenant of salt?"

The economic significance of salt can be gauged from the part it played in developing trade relations between countries, for example, between south Russia and Greece in the early days of the Greek city states, when the salt pans at the mouth of the river Dniester promoted the growth of a salted fish industry, which in turn attracted the attention of Greek traders. Again, in the Roman world, clear evidence may be cited of the impact of salt on the lives of ordinary men and women. The Via Salaria, the Salt Road, was one of the oldest roads of Italy, running up country from the salt pans of Ostia, near Rome, while in the Roman army all ranks received an allowance of salt, which was later commuted to a sum of money, known as salarium, from which the English word "salary" is derived. When the Romans, who settled in Britain in 43 AD, moved north into Cheshire, they found there was already a thriving salt industry thereabouts. Brine springs abounded in the Northwich area. The Romans improved upon existing production methods by introducting the open-pan system of evaporation which became the accepted way of obtaining salt until more modern methods overtook it in the twentieth century.

Just how important salt became in the lives of communities can be judged from the regulation and taxation of salt supplies enforced by many governments. While most countries in Europe possess plenty of salt, there are particularly large deposits in England, Germany and Poland. Governments tended either to impose very heavy taxes on it or sometimes even to corner it as a state monopoly. In France, the gabelle became probably the most resented of all taxes; it was first imposed as long ago as in 1286, becoming later a state monopoly which stayed in force until abolished by the revolutionary government in 1790. Under the gabelle laws every person in France over the age of eight was compelled to buy every week a minimum quantity of salt at a price which was regulated by the government, while those who are familiar with the history of India will need no reminding of the part played there by the government-maintained salt tax in preparing the minds of Indians for seeking a breach with their rulers.

In the history of England salt has often played a vital role; for, while today it may still seem to many of us highly desirable, until the middle of the eighteenth century its rôle was even more basically essential. From the time that farming was developed as a key economic factor in English life, farmers were faced with the annual problem of knowing what to do with their livestock in the autumn. In the absence of any winter feed for cattle, there was a wholesale slaughter every autumn. A few hardy animals were somehow fed and kept alive through the winter months to enable the farmers to renew their stock the following spring. The slaughtered carcasses had to be salted down to provide a winter supply of meat; this meat supply became even more valuable when in the later middle ages the widespread import of spices from the East enabled the discerning and the prosperous to camouflage the unpleasant taste in late winter of meat that had been salted down, often inadequately, several months previously.

The problem was considerably eased eventually by the cultivation of the turnip as a field crop; this invaluable vegetable, which was to provide the necessary winter feed for cattle, had been introduced into England as a garden crop in the reign of Charles II and spread to the countryside of East Anglia in the first half of the eighteenth century. From that time the autumn slaughter gradually declined but certainly as late as in 1703, when the price of salt in England was increased, there was a general outcry resulting in a petition being sent to Parliament, demanding action on the grounds that 'it was a grievance to the poorer sort of people who mostly feed on salted provisions'. An important by-product of the ending of the annual cattle slaughter was the rapid expansion of the size of the herds. The increased food supply was thus able to satisfy the requirements of the new populations brought about by the growth of the factory towns.

A hundred years ago there was a general acceptance in this country of the verdict of Mrs Beeton, when she wrote: "The importance of salt cannot be overestimated. Salt is indispensable." While few today would deny that salt is still required in cooking, the over-reliance on it in the preparation of convenience foods and the increased medical knowledge of the damage salt may do to the heart have caused dietary experts and doctors to counsel the general public about the dangerous consequences of over-indulgence. However, whatever the rights and wrongs as to the correct use of salt today, no-one would query the historic value of salt throughout the past three thousand years.

Pericles

In 433 BC war broke out between Athens and her great rival, Sparta;
three years later an outbreak of bubonic plague seriously weakened
Athens and in 429 Pericles, their leader, died of the disease.
His death did much to sap the morale of the Athenians, who were
eventually beaten by Sparta in 404 BC.

Bubonic Plague

It is ironical that the course of history should several times have
been changed by the action of one of the smallest organisms in
nature, a bacillus carried by a flea that rode on the back of the black
rat, whose blood it sucked — not that our forefathers suspected
this happening; indeed, no-one knew the cause of the great
pestilence though Gibbon in the middle of the eighteenth century
hazarded a guess that it was an African fever which "is generated
from the putrefaction of animal substances". He rather thought
that dead locusts were largely responsible.

There certainly was a general assocation of the disease with pollution and the smells that accompanied pollution; it was also noted that the disease entered a country through a port and rapidly spread inland. It was widely believed that to take protective action against the smells was a sensible precaution; hence a variety of pleasant odours was called into use, especially those belonging to flowers. Indeed, it was a common practice to sniff a bunch of sweetly-scented flowers when approaching ill-smelling areas. That judges on assize normally carried posies of flowers served to provide a salutary reminder of the dangers to which they were exposed when the plague was an occupational hazard.

The old nursery rhyme "Ring a ring o' roses, A pocket full of posies, Atishoo, atishoo, All fall down" tells a graphic story. A circular red ring on the body was often an early sign of the onset of the plague which in this particular case had not been prevented by the possession of a posy of flowers. A bout of sneezing frequently followed, which all too often and all too quickly gave notice of impending death. From Greek times onwards sneezing was thought an unhappy omen, which might well herald an attack of the plague. Hence when a Greek sneezed, even though it might only be a sign of the common cold, his friends would always bow, in order to placate the gods, while Romans prayed and early Christians said "God bless you". It is even possible that some readers of these words may have formed the habit of saying "Bless you", when they hear someone sneeze!

The plague intervened in Greek affairs in the fifth century BC, which was the heyday of the city-state. Sixty years previously Athens had taken the lead among its rival city-states by organising successful resistance to the Persians who were trying to establish a foothold in Europe. This successful alliance of free states under the guidance of Athens in the years that followed became an Athenian empire, whose members, it must be said, seem to have been for the most part willing participants. The opportunity provided the right man, Pericles, under whose aegis the Parthenon was built in the middle of the fifth century; in the Theatre of Dionysius under the Acropolis were at the same time being performed the plays of Aeschylus, Sophocles and Euripides before enthusiastic audiences, which were made aware of the interaction of Hubris and Nemesis, of arrogance and retribution in human affairs. This imaginative Greek personification of the moral law, which in later Christian times was postulated as "whatsoever a man sows that shall he also reap", quickened the Athenian conscience. Many thoughtful Athenians thereafter became disturbed as they looked around and saw their city overreaching itself. Such hubris, it was believed, would surely be followed by retribution. In 433 the power of Athens was challenged by that of Sparta and war resulted. While the Athenian navy was all-powerful at sea, the armies of Sparta were able to emerge from the Peloponnese and with impunity raid the country districts around Athens, whose inhabitants had to become evacuees inside the walls that had been previously built to join Athens to its port of Peiraeus.

In 430 ships from Egypt brought the plague to the Peiraeus, where it claimed its first victim before spreading with alarming speed through the overcrowded ranks of the refugees inside the walls, and on to Athens itself. So terrible was the loss of human life in this outbreak that the military strength of Athens was seriously weakened but, worse still, was the effect that the disaster had on the Athenian mentality. Nemesis had struck, men believed; Athens was being punished for her previous acts of arrogance. In this dangerous mood of self-questioning the will to win was undermined and when in the next year Pericles himself died of the plague, their cup of misery was full. Had Winston Churchill died in 1940 at the height of the Battle of Britain the effect on British morale might well have been similar. Although in fact Athens did not finally capitulate to Sparta until 404 BC, never again after the death of Pericles did the light of victory shine in Athenian eyes. The black rat proved to be Sparta's unknown ally.

This epidemic of bubonic plague in Greece in the fifth century BC was no isolated occurrence; that so much is known about it is due solely to the fact that the Athenian historian Thucydides, having himself survived an attack of the disease, yet managed to write an objective account of it. That there were other such outbreaks and that they were the scourge of mankind there can be little doubt. The next authenticated account came in the sixth century AD, when the Prefect of Constantinople, the capital of the eastern Roman Empire, was none other than the historian Procopius, who served the great emperor Justinian. The whole of Europe was ravaged as a series of epidemics spread inland from various ports. During one period of three months in Constantinople it is said that ten thousand people died every day. It is known from Procopius that the disease reached Constantinople in 542, to which must be added the conclusion of Gibbon: "It was not," he wrote, "until the end of the calamitous period of fifty two years that mankind recovered its health and the air resumed its pure and salubrious quality." In the seventh century Bede wrote of outbreaks of pestilence in England in five different years, but the accounts are not sufficiently detailed to allow a certain diagnosis, although the epidemic of 690 AD appears to have been of bubonic plague.

Little is known about the frequency of these epidemics; it is however a reasonable surmise that, as travelling in western Europe increased with the opening-up of trade routes following the Crusades, the outbreaks accordingly grew in numbers until the fourteenth century when a great peak was reached. In the first half of that century the Black Death swept through Europe like a fire out of control; in 1348 it struck Jersey and Guernsey with devastating results and from there reached the mainland near Weymouth from whence it was all too soon claiming victims in Devonshire, Somerset and Bristol. By 1349 it had penetrated the whole country and the following year, crossed into Scotland.

Everywhere the loss of life was greatest in the towns, presumably because the filth and insanitary conditions in overcrowded areas encouraged the black rat. Estimates of the loss of life vary considerably; a conservative figure is that one third of the entire population of England and Wales died. It is known that in one London cemetery in 1349 fifty thousand were buried, while the number of lives lost in the whole of Europe from bubonic plague in the course of the fourteenth century amounted to no less than twenty five millions. The 1348 outbreak in these islands was followed by other epidemics, not quite as disastrous but still terrible enough, in 1361, 1362 and in 1369.

The fourteenth century in England is thought of as a great century of change; even before the catastrophe of the Black Death in the middle of the century, the peasants had grown more determined in their resolve to resist what they regarded as excessive demands from their landlords, but their great number had made any immediate improvement in their lot unlikely. This glut of labour was swiftly turned into a shortage through the ravages of the disease. In consequence the laws of supply and demand began to work dramatically in favour of the peasants who found they could for a while get almost any wage they asked. Landlords, caught in the bewildering change of events and forced by circumstances to pay higher wages, raised the rents. Whereupon a great many labourers decamped in search of other employers who were prepared to meet their demands, if they wanted their crops planted and harvested. Landowners at this time had a clear majority in the House of Commons and in consequence forced through Parliament in 1351 the Statute of Labourers which attempted to force back wages to their pre Black Death level, but the act had little effect. One great result of the Black Death then in England was greatly to improve the conditions of the peasants; other less dramatic consequences were a decline in the monastic movement, as thousands of monks died of the plague, and the cessation in the middle of the century, through shortage of craftsmen, of the building of new churches and cathedrals, thus limiting the achievements of those who built in the Decorated style.

In the following century outbreaks of the plague still occurred but at no time engulfed the whole country as in 1348. Throughout the fifteenth and sixteenth centuries different parts of the country at different times suffered from the unwelcome visitor and once again it was particularly the towns that had to play host to the black rat and his fleas. In the seventeenth century the situation improved in so far that there were longer intervals between the epidemics; nevertheless, both in 1604 and in 1626, at the coronations of the first two Stuart kings, the celebrations were darkened by coincidental serious outbreaks of the plague in the capital. The next and, as things turned out, the last really serious epidemic came to London in 1665, having been spared the disease during the civil war. Not all parts of the country were as fortunate during the 1640s — Chester even lost a quarter of its population between 1642 and 1646.

What Thucydides did for the plague in Athens and Procopius did for it in Constantinople, Samuel Pepys was to do for it in London. The pestilence was first reported early in June 1665, having travelled speedily from Holland with whom England was at war. On June 7th Pepys wrote: " . . . the hottest day that ever I felt in my life . . . this day I did in Drury Lane see two or three houses marked with a red cross upon the doors and 'Lord have mercy upon us' writ there . . . I was forced to buy some roll tobacco to smell . . . which took away the apprehension." Ten days later on June 17th, the entry reads: " . . . it struck me very deep this afternoon, going with a hackney coach down Holborn, the coachman . . . at last stood still and came down, hardly able to stand and told me that he was suddenly struck very sick and almost blind . . . " On June 21st Pepys wrote: "I find the coaches and wagons being all full of people going into the country." The entry for August 31st added: " . . . in the city this week six thousand one hundred and two people died of the plague but it is feared that the true number is near ten thousand; partly from the poor that cannot be taken notice of through the greatness of their numbers, and partly from the Quakers and others that will not have any bell ring for them." This disastrous pattern of events was repeated up and down the country throughout that hot summer but with the coming of colder weather in the autumn, the casualty rate slackened but as late as in the following March, Pepys reported that the weekly death rate for the plague in London still exceeded forty. For a very graphic account of the 1665 outbreak of plague the reader is recommended to read Daniel Defoe's *A Journal of the Plague Year*, even though, seeing that the author was only six years of age at the time, the narrative must owe more to hearsay than to memory. The facts, however, speak for themselves; of London's population in 1665 of about four hundred and sixty thousand, almost three hundred thousand fled to the country; of the remainder, seventy thousand died. After the pestilence came the fire. London started to burn early in September 1666.

After 1665 the plague never again presented Londoners with such nightmarish conditions, though there were sporadic, if much less serious, outbreaks. This beneficent change prompted some observers to credit the fire with responsibility for removing the causes of the disease. While it certainly is true that in the new buildings in London brick was used instead of mud and wood, and that carpets on wooden floors encouraged rats less than straw had done, the decline in the frequency and virulence of the plague had a more fundamental reason.

Very gradually, living conditions improved but it was not until after the first Public Health Act in 1848 that sewers were built and it took another twenty years before sanitation generally in this country became anything like reasonable. This slow amelioration of sanitary conditions cannot therefore be the main reason why the plague claimed fewer victims, because even in the eighteenth century when conditions were still very bad, the impact of the disease was far less than in the previous century. Indeed, Man can take little credit for this change of affairs. Nature, as so often unpredictable and inexorable, gives the answer. From about the end of the seventeenth century in western Europe the brown rat began to multiply at the expense of the black rat and happily for mankind there were no bacilli-carrying fleas on brown rats.

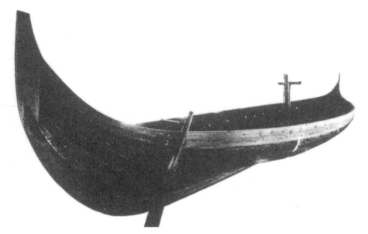

A Viking Ship   (reconstruction)

Vikings

The Vikings, like the Romans before them, had a bad Press! Just as the Romans came and saw and conquered in the public mind, so did the Vikings spread terror far and wide when they crept silently up the creeks on dark nights. Admittedly the Romans were military conquerors and the Vikings were bloodthirsty sea raiders but there was much more to the Romans than fighting and much more to the Vikings than raiding. As far as this country was concerned, the Roman legions began to leave at the beginning of the 5th century AD and the Vikings first made their presence felt towards the end of the eighth century.

The vacuum left by the Roman withdrawal was to be filled by Saxons, Angles and Jutes from north Germany and Jutland in the fifth century; the years 400-600 AD were years of great uncertainty, still wreathed in clouds of mystery, where fact and fiction overlap. Of Arthur and Vortigern much has been written but really very little is known. The Roman towns were abandoned as most of Britain's inhabitants went rural again with the Saxons. Shortly before the year 600, St Augustine was sent by the Pope to bring back Christianity to the eastern parts of the country, Ethelbert, the King of Kent, becoming the first Saxon king to be converted to Christianity. In the following century Christianity spread north from Kent into East Anglia and up into Northumbria. The eighth century was a time of peace and promise; it was the time of a great historian, Bede, and of the Lindisfarne Gospels, of the great cross at Bewcastle, and of the gentle scholar Alcuin, but before the century was out, storm cones were to be hoisted on the east coast. The peace and culture were ruptured by the stealthy approach of the Vikings. The raids from Scandinavia were about to begin.

Who indeed were these Vikings and where did they come from? Their far-off homes were in the northern lands, where today there live the Norwegians, the Swedes and the Danes. In some parts of Europe they were known as the Northmen or the Norsemen, and in other parts, the Vikings, but to every one they were, one and all, raiders and destroyers, restless and ruthless seamen, who were also wonderful navigators. Their various expeditions took them to Spain and to Italy, to Iceland and to Russia, to France and to our own islands. Europe was once again at the mercy of adventurers and conquerors. The power of Rome had long since gone and when the great and good Charlemagne, who had built securely in the west, creating an empire based on Christian law and order, died in 814, his influence soon ebbed and the empire he had built crumbled and disintegrated. The men from the north saw their chance and took it.

Their most spectacular conquests were in the east and the west. The Swedes moved along the rivers of Russia, sailing the Volga and the Dnieper and establishing themselves at Kiev. Meanwhile, men from Norway and Denmark were raiding and colonising with equal success in the west; some of their number landed and settled in the north of France in 911, calling their conquest Normandy. In addition, many of those who went to Iceland made settlements there; a great deal is known about their civilisation and culture up there from the Icelandic sagas of which the most important and probably the most worth reading today is the story of Burnt Njal. From these bases in Iceland Viking ships managed to cross the north Atlantic, enabling colonies to be set up in North America six hundred years before Christopher Columbus made his historic voyage.

These same northern Vikings raided and settled in the Faroes, Shetland, the Orkneys, in the Hebrides and in various parts of mainland Scotland, north and south, in Northumbria, Cumbria and Lancashire, in the Isle of Man and in Ireland. Of many of these raids very little is known; enough of the consequences have survived however to realise that the very fabric of civilisation in western Europe, already greatly weakened, was very nearly ruined by them. This is particularly true of Ireland, where the impact was probably the severest of all.

Ireland, which had escaped Saxon infiltration and conquest, was enjoying a secure and trouble-free existence, with a separate and exciting culture, when the Viking raids began. This golden age of Ireland came to a sudden and terrible end in 853, when the Vikings, as the result of an overwhelming military victory, became the lords of Ireland. This overlordship was to last for more than a century and a half; the Irish monasteries were destroyed, their treasures looted and dispersed, but settlement eventually followed the destruction and the commercial prosperity associated in later days with Dublin, Wexford, Waterford and Limerick stemmed from these Viking origins.

One of the most deplorable results of Viking expansion in this area was the destruction of Iona, through which hallowed island Christianity had flowed from Irish monasteries to Christianised parts of southern Scotland and north-east England. All the islands captured off the west coast of Scotland and as far south as the Isle of Man the Vikings called the Sudreys, meaning the Southern Islands. An echo of this early name survives in the title of the bishop who is still responsible for the spiritual welfare of the Isle of Man; he is known as the Bishop of Sodor and Man.

Scotland in the ninth century was the unwilling recipient of continuous Viking penetration; in 839 the Picts were thoroughly routed in battle and even possibly exterminated as a race. At any rate, the Picts thereafter disappeared from the written record. From that time there was so much Viking settlement in various parts of Scotland, but especially in the islands of the north and west and along the east coast, that Viking blood became an important contributary constituent in the Scottish race. Shetland and the Orkneys, the very heartland of the Vikings in the west, remained politically part of a Norse empire until as late as 1469, when these islands were at last incorporated in Scotland.

In England, the Viking threat came from the Danes who infiltrated into eastern parts of the country at the time when Egbert, the King of Wessex (802-839), enjoyed the overlordship of Northumbria and Mercia, which the Danes were soon to undermine. Egbert's son, Ethelwulf (839-858), was even less successful in dealing with the intruders, while in the reign of his son, Ethelbert, Winchester itself suffered the ignominy of a Danish sacking in 860. At about this time the invaders seem to have taken the historic decision to follow up conquest here with settlement; certainly in 867 a great concentration of Danes massed in Yorkshire, which virtually became a Danish kingdom, while three years later another of their armies moved into East Anglia which they overran after killing their king, Edmund. The Danes were then ready to square up to their main antagonists, the men of Wessex, against whom the first attack was launched in 871. Initial successful resistance from Wessex caused the Danes to postpone any further assault until they had overcome the Mercians, whose lands lay between their early conquests and Wessex. By 878 the issue was clear; the great struggle was about to begin between the Danes and Wessex, now ruled by the young Alfred, who had succeeded to his dominions in the critical year of 871, when only twenty-three years of age.

This young king of Wessex, faced as he was by such a Herculean task, became, by his stout resistance and by his subsequent statesmanship, the only one of our rulers ever to acquire the title of "the Great". He met the Danish army under Guthrum at the Battle of Chippenham, where he gave a sufficiently good account of himself to force the Danish leader to agree to the terms of the Treaty of Wedmore, whereby Alfred was left in control of western Mercia and those parts of England which were south of the river Thames. Nevertheless, although Guthrum had agreed to make no further attack against Wessex, the Danes were left in possession of more than half the country. In this Danelaw, as it was called, the former fighting men settled down to become peaceful citizens, though of a country quite separate from the rest of England.

Early in the tenth century, however, Alfred's son, Edward the Elder, recovered the rest of Mercia and east Anglia and by 924 the southern boundary of the Danelaw had become the river Humber. Athelstan, who succeeded Edward in 939, moved further north and rescued Yorkshire and Lancashire from the Danes so that by the middle of the century the political hold of the Danes here had been broken, though of course there was by now a great deal of Viking blood in those who lived in the east and north of England, just as there was also in the inhabitants of the north and east of Scotland.

The whole story of Viking conquest in this country has not yet however been fully told because in a period of utter anarchy in England towards the end of the tenth century, the Danes once more returned. This time they came in such numbers and took such advantage of the prevailing chaos that in 1016 there was a Danish king on the throne of England and England became a part of a great northern empire, which included Norway and Denmark. The king's name was Canute and he ruled the country wisely and well until his death in 1035; his two sons, who in quick succession followed him, proved to be quite inadequate rulers so that in 1042 the wheel of fortune turned once more. The Danish empire collapsed and the crown of England was assumed by Edward the Confessor until his death in January 1066, when the Saxon Harold began his short but memorable reign.

Earlier in this chapter mention was made of the settlement in 911 of men from the north in northern France, where they conquered and settled down and in the course of the following century succeeded in making their land one of the best-organised communities in Western Europe. These Christianised Northmen became the Normans, whose culture was already permeating large areas of southern England in the reign of Edward the Confessor, whose mother indeed had been a Norman. When the throne of England fell vacant at Edward's death in January 1066, the Normans felt that they had a strong claim to the succession. The immediate opportunity passed with the accession of Harold, but not the desire nor the intention on the part of the Normans to make good their claim to the English throne at some future date.

A month before Harold had to face this Norman attempt to renew its claim to the English throne, he had had to beat off another Viking threat, when Harold Hardrada, the King of Norway, invaded east Yorkshire. On the 25th of September Harold managed to throw back this Viking invasion at the Battle of Stamford Bridge, just east of the city of York, only to discover a week later that the Normans had landed in Sussex. The rest is history; the Vikings had at long last made good their conquest of England, but these Vikings had already accepted the religion and the culture of western Europe.

By way of postscript, the happy fact has to recorded that in April 1984 there opened in York the Jorvic Viking Centre, where, by a truly remarkable exercise in imaginative historical reconstruction, life in a tenth century Viking settlement has been recreated. The emphasis in York is not on war and conquest but on the conditions of the everyday life of ordinary men and women. The exhibition's time capsule enables visitors in the late twentieth century to go back into tenth century Viking shops and houses and to see replicas of the artifacts in general use at the time, to the accompaniment of contemporary sounds and even smells. In addition to the experience of being moved back into the social life of a thousand years ago, there are also on view a great many Viking objects, which do much to make meaningful the history of a very important part of the Danelaw.

A Medieval Guildhall

Guilds

England after 1066 was dramatically reorganised; the King became the supreme feudal overlord, to whom lesser Norman lords owed allegiance, who in turn exacted allegiance from other lesser lords. At every step in this feudal process downtrodden Saxon peasants commended themselves, that is to say, accepted a relationship with local landlords. Thereafter, in return for working several days a week on their lords' lands, the peasants received food and protection. This early feudal society, based on land tenure, became tightly-knit and all-embracing, a society in which at first there were only two classes, those who owned the land and those who worked it. Gradually however small towns grew, which soon attracted the attention of Norman lords, who forced their inhabitants to pay feudal dues to them. In the long run, however, as the towns became stronger and more powerful, their leaders managed to defy their landlords and in very many cases regained their independence.

The large sums of money with which the towns bought off their feudal lords were contributed by the minority of wealthy citizens, who comprised the corporate bodies. They for their part on the morrow of acquiring their independence had no intention of sharing the privileges won by their wealth and leadership with the other inhabitants of the towns, who had made no contribution to the enterprise; instead they formed themselves into merchant guilds, which were to make themselves responsible for every branch of urban life and activity.

Merchant guilds first appeared in England as early as in the eleventh century and gradually thereafter town government of all but London and one or two other large towns passed completely into their hands. In the course of time, having firmly established their position of power, these guilds made themselves responsible for all the trade and commerce of the towns, indeed for every aspect of town government; they controlled all buying and selling and gradually admitted to their ranks all the craftsmen of the town, who, whatever their trade, belonged to the one guild merchant. The chief aims of these guilds were to maintain the privileges and monopolies of their members and to prevent anyone else from having a share in the benefits they enjoyed. All members had to pay an entrance fee, which provided a merchant guild with the necessary revenue. Four special advantages were enjoyed by members. They received a share in the profits of trade, they were made exempt from the payment of the many tolls to which others were subject, they alone were authorised to sell the wares they made, thus eliminating all competition and finally, they had a vital say in the way in which their towns were governed.

Supreme authority was usually in the hands of aldermen, who were assisted by two or three wardens. The members of the guild met periodically in the guildhall, where they dined together before discussing future plans and policies. On these occasions in addition to electing new officers, where required, and admitting new members, members of the guild, who had fallen foul of the strict rules of the guild, were brought up for trial and punishment.

In one way the very success that attended the efforts of the merchant guilds contributed to their eventual supersession by another form of organisation, the craft guilds. As long as towns remained small and compact, a merchant guild could efficiently control all its trades and industries, but as trade and industry expanded and attracted more merchants and craftsmen to the town, the merchant guilds became too big and too unwieldy. Furthermore, it became extremely difficult for one body to regulate the details of an increasing range of economic activities. When this happened (as it frequently did in the thirteenth century), the various crafts started to organise themselves separately. Discontent had also been growing for some time in the ranks of many craftsmen, who felt that they were not receiving adequate rewards for their labours. It came to be suspected, and with some reason, that the leaders of some merchant guilds were in close contact with their opposite numbers in merchant guilds in other towns. As a consequence it was believed by the malcontents that the leaders were acting together in such matters as fixing the price to be paid to the craftsmen in their respective towns, driving very hard bargains which craftsmen at first resented and later resisted.

The segregation of craftsmen into separate craft guilds began much earlier on the continent than here, the first one probably being the candlemakers' guild which was formed in Paris in 1091. Probably the earliest in this country were in the middle of the twelfth century when certain craftsmen in London, Oxford and elsewhere, who were engaged in weaving and fulling wool, set up craft guilds. Some of the early craft guilds met with opposition from existing merchant guilds but in general in England, though not on the continent, there was little active illwill between the merchant and craft guilds. The plain fact was that it had become impossible in the rapidly-expanding towns for the existing merchant guilds to do all that was required of them in seeing to the needs of every branch of trade and industry. Amongst the most popular craft guilds were those that represented weavers and fullers, shoemakers, bakers, spinners, dyers and millers. In some towns there were more than fifty separate craft guilds; it has also to be said that, whereas merchant guilds in different towns sometimes acted together for their mutual benefit, there was no such relationship at all between the craft guild for a particular trade in one town and a similar craft guild in another.

In our society today much stress is laid upon individual rights and privileges, but individualism is a comparatively recent phenomenon that came with the Renaissance, which first affected attitudes in this country in the sixteenth century. In the middle ages there were certain jealously-guarded rights and privileges, and obligations too, but those all arose from membership of a group. There was a very strong sense of group consciousness, within which individuals were able to enjoy freedom. Nowhere was the importance of this sense of common purpose and group awareness more apparent than in the conduct of the craft guilds. As members of a craft guild lived and worked near each other, they naturally comprised a compact social group; many a medieval town in England still proclaims its former connection with craft guilds in the names of their streets, e.g. Shoe Lane, Bread Street, Wood Street etc.

Within a group were to be found both employers and employees, master craftsmen and apprentices. The minimum period of an apprenticeship was seven years (for a goldsmith it was ten); the apprentice, at the expiry of his training, had to make an article to show that he had learned his trade. This was his 'masterpiece' and if it was passed as being up to standard, the apprentice became a journeyman. As such he was allowed to work for others (and be paid by the day) but not to be his own master. That in later years so many journeymen were unable to become master craftsmen was a source of increasing irritation and friction. All members of the guild elected from their own number a ruler, known as the Warden, whose overall responsibility was to maintain standards. Among his specific duties were those of punishing cheating in the trade and of appointing Searchers to examine all work done and put up for sale by members of the guild.

Each guild had a fund to which every member had to make an

annual contribution. Members who fell ill or were too old to work or who suffered some sudden and unexpected misfortune, received financial help from this fund, an insurance scheme which did much to tighten the social cohesion of the guild. In addition when a member died, his widow was helped financially by the guild and spiritually by the guild chaplain, who was himself a paid official. Each guild also employed a clerk and a cook, the services of the latter being much in demand when guild feasts were held. On festive occasions, such as the feast days of the guild's patron saint, all members were expected to attend church for the celebration of a solemn mass before going in procession to the guildhall for the feast, which was very often followed by a play performed by members of the guild.

Above all, craft guilds stood or fell by the quality of the work of their members over whom a strict control could be exercised through the tightly-integrated living and working arrangements. A guild, as well as protecting its members against outside craftsmen, regulated every detail of work inside the guild, where it had absolute control of the quality of the craftsmanship. To put bad material into an article was regarded as a very serious offence, which was punished on the first occasion by a fine and subsequently by expulsion from the guild. The guild also fixed the price, insisting on what was thought of as a 'fair price' that is to say, the cost of the materials used and what the warden considered a reasonable profit for making the article. No-one was allowed to make a shortage of goods a justifiable reason for claiming extra profit.

Members of craft guilds generally accepted considerable responsibility for the welfare of the towns in which they worked, undertaking valuable voluntary duties such as repairing roads and bridges, at a time when there was no statutory arrangement for such vital maintenance. Sometimes they also paid towards the upkeep of schools, chantries and almshouses as well as providing public entertainment with their staging of mystery plays. By the fourteenth century most craft guilds were at their peak of achievement; by then every trade of any size in a big town had its own craft guild.

Success brings problems; an institution grows and thereby changes its character. As the craft guilds became more prosperous, so did the original cohesion tend to grow looser. Whereas in earlier days all members shared a common sense of purpose, whether they were masters, journeymen or apprentices, with the expansion of trade and the increasing prosperity of some guilds, internal distinctions became more marked; there was a greater diversification of functions as well as widely differing financial rewards. The most prosperous master craftsmen tended to spend less time making their wares and more time selling them, thus distancing themselves from the place of work. At the same time, resentment was growing at the lack of opportunities for promotion within the guild, where only a comparatively small number of journeymen managed to attain the grade of master craftsman. By the middle of the fourteenth century the old pattern of the craft guilds, where masters and men shared a common purpose, was beginning to break; a new connotation of employers and employees was taking its place. There were differences too between masters where some, as they grew rich, became entrepreneurs, while others remained in the workshop, where with a few journeymen they pursued their traditional ways.

The growing clash of economic interests led to considerable internal dissension; there were even occasional strikes aimed at getting higher wages but as this form of expressing workers' grievances produced few tangible results, more drastic action was attempted. In consequence in many parts of western Europe, but more particularly in Germany, there was a large-scale breakaway movement. Here in England small masters joined forces with dissatisfied journeymen and together formed a number of separate guilds, which came to be known as yeoman or bachelor guilds. The resulting conflict between master craftsmen in their craft guilds and the journeymen and their allies in the yeoman guilds resembled a modern struggle between employers and workers, especially as the commonest grounds of complaint concerned rates of pay and hours of work. It would be wrong, however, to exaggerate the seriousness of the split in English craft guilds; the yeoman guilds were not many in number nor were they conspicuously successful.

Change nevertheless was in the air; the old order no longer corresponded to the requirements of a new age. When, towards the end of the fourteenth century, society in England was convulsed by civil unrest in the Peasants' Revolt in 1381, it was perhaps significant that many members of the craft guilds threw in their lot with the peasants, while some unpopular members of merchant guilds shared the fate of many landowners. Nevertheless, taking the long view, both merchant and craft guilds were on the side of freedom; they may not always have agreed with each other but, when faced by an external threat of tyranny, they displayed a stubborn resistance. It has to be remembered too that in after years, it was the towns of England which proved the undoing of Charles I. By then, of course, the guilds had decayed but the spirit that had quickened them lived on and helped to lay the firm foundations of our modern society.

Narrow fields created by the enclosure of medieval field-strips near Tideswell, Derbyshire

Enclosures

Before dealing with the circumstances that accompanied the growth of enclosures, something must first be said about the agricultural system it was to supersede. From Anglo-Saxon times there were a great many village communities in England, surrounding which were two or three very large open fields, each of which was divided into many strips of land. The separate open fields were, as a rule, marked off from each other by movable wooden barriers. The village meeting would allocate to each individual peasant a certain number of strips which were always scattered throughout the different fields. Although these strips were individually worked, the crops grown there and the animals pastured there were controlled by the village community. This system in a rough and ready way was just and even economically sound, as long as the only need for the individual cultivator of his strips was to satisfy the needs of his family. The position however became more complicated over the years as feudal practices grew and developed. G.M. Trevelyan in his *English Social History* makes this point: "On this democracy of peasant cultivators was heavily superimposed the feudal power and legal rights of the lord of the manor". The individual who worked his strips was a free and equal members of the village community but at the same time he was also a serf, at the beck and call of the lord of the manor, who exacted from him a variety of services which took up a good deal of his working life.

Came the fourteenth century with its Black Death, to be followed by the Statute of Labourers and the Peasants' Revolt, but even before the full impact of the Black Death was felt, many peasants had managed to change their relationship to the lord of the manor from that of serf to tenant, by getting the lord to agree to accept from them rent instead of services. This tendency was greatly accelerated after the middle of the century, when the enormous loss of life in the Black Death brought about a serious shortage of labour, which, despite the intention of the Statute of Labourers to put the clock back, resulted in very many peasants leaving home in order to work for other masters who were prepared to pay the wages demanded without charging exorbitant rents for the houses provided for their workers. The fourteenth century brought about significant changes on the land, not the least of these being the improvement in the lot of the peasants.

The dawn of the fifteenth century, however, was to prove a false one for the English peasantry because just when their conditions had undergone a marked improvement their prospects were blighted by the arrival on the agricultural scene of a new social class, the members of which were to apply in the countryside those capitalist methods that had proved so successful in organising trade in the towns. Until that time the feudal landowners, the lords of the manor in the middle ages, had regarded the land primarily as a commodity which would provide them with an adequate supply of man power, to be used in peace time for working the land and in war for accompanying them in battle. In the fifteenth century their place was largely taken by prosperous traders who came to regard the land as an investment to be developed along business lines. As a result, with capital available for the first time for agricultural development, the pattern of the rural past was broken, to be replaced by an entirely new situation, which was to follow the enclosure of land. The whole of rural society was about to be restructured.

Many books have been written about enclosures, in which quite different opinions have been forcibly expressed. By the fifteenth century far-reaching changes in agriculture had to come; there were more mouths to be fed and there were on hand men with the knowledge and the money to bring these changes about. Strips of land that had survived from the three field system were often enclosed, that is to say, were fenced around or walled in by the new landlords after they had either bought them or annexed them if the previous occupants had decamped; such enclosures were very often made in order to convert arable land into pasture, though frequently much of the newly-acquired land had lain out of use for a very long time. This type of enclosure was widespread but not confined entirely to the new capitalist farmers, as sometimes small yeomen who had resisted the temptation to decamp to improve themselves elsewhere and had stayed on, gradually added to their own strips the no longer used strips of others. These they now fenced in and turned into small compact farms.

In addition much enclosure also took place of common land, which whether consisting of woodland or rough pasture, comprised a vital part of the village community in the middle ages. All those who had strips in the open fields also had rights on the common land, where beasts might be grazed, turf cut or wood obtained to keep the homes fires burning. Long before the middle ages ended, encroachment on the common land had started and had become a very serious bone of contention between the peasants and the would-be new owners. In the fifteenth and later centuries there was wholesale enclosure of common land, some of which was used for the growing of crops, but as the profit margin was much greater in wool production, most of the former common land was used for pasture. In the fifteenth and sixteenth centuries enclosures, whether of surviving strips of the open field system or of village common land or of forest and waste land, previously thought incapable of cultivation, succeeded in greatly increasing the agricultural wealth of this country.

The social consequences that attended these fundamental changes were considerable; the effects of turning arable land into pasture were inescapable, as one man and his dog were able to look after a great many sheep on a very large pasture. Hence, however legal, however economically desirable such enclosures may have been, the economic consequences for the dispossessed were appalling. According to one estimate made in the middle of the sixteenth century, ten per cent of the whole population had been put out of work through the enclosures made for sheep grazing; the actual number cited was three hundred thousand. The English wool trade made enormous profits but many thousands of previously settled peasants became nomadic and joined the ever-increasing army of "beggars", who seem to have been a permanent feature of life in Tudor England. Even fiercer resentment was felt over the enclosures of common land; the social damage done may have been far less but the sense of injustice rankled. It was encapsulated in a popular rhyme:

> The law locks up the man or woman
> Who steals the goose from off the common
> But leaves the greater felon loose
> Who steals the common from the goose.

The enclosure movement proceeded slowly in the seventeenth century, when not interrupted altogether by civil unrest, but in the eighteenth it gathered such momentum that it succeeded in breaking up the very structure of our village communities. Much land at the beginning of the century remained unenclosed and therefore economically unprofitable. The agricultural methods practised there were primitive in the extreme, the yield from crops was small, and sheep and cattle were of a very poor quality, at a time when the population was growing apace, especially in the new towns. It was essential that there should be more enclosure but unhappily much of it resembled surgery without anaesthetics. The procedure still in use for enclosing land was by local agreement, despite the attempt made by Parliament in an act of 1709 to encourage the petitioning of Parliament by a would-be encloser. Another fifty years were to elapse before private acts of Parliament became the normal means of enclosing land.

One of the stimuli which helped to bring about more efficient agricultural methods and which therefore made more enclosure necessary, was the spirit of scientific enquiry that was abroad in the eighteenth century, an intellectual awareness, which had been encouraged by the foundation of the Royal Society in the reign of Charles II, that fitted in neatly with the stark economic need to feed the rapidly expanding population. Hence, while in the previous centuries enclosures had largely been decided upon by the need to encourage sheep farming and production of more wool, enclosure in the eighteenth century aimed at improving agriculture generally through mixed farming and a better rotation of crops. In the course of the century the supply of wheat showed a marked increase and sheep were being bred primarily for mutton rather than for wool. Changes in the rotation of crops, more knowledge of the manuring of the land, increasing expertness in stockbreeding, better methods of sowing, the building of more suitable farm buildings, the making of farm roads, — these and other such advances in the eighteenth century demanded much extra capital and in time were responsible for what amounted to an agricultural revolution. Thus it was that the factory workers in the swollen towns, many of whose parents a generation previously had worked on the land, were supplied with food.

With the pressure increasing for more enclosures there was recourse by the middle of the eighteenth century to drawing up private petitions to Parliament. The procedure was this. A farmer who wanted to enclose land drew up a petition which his local Member of Parliament presented to Parliament; in this petition the disadvantages of the existing situation were fully set out along with the advantages which would be expected to accrue from an enclosure. Parliament, if it approved the petition, gave permission for a bill to be presented. The next step was the formal first reading, followed by the second; the bill was then referred to a committee, which had to listen to any representations that might be made by those who opposed the enclosure. The changes recommended by the committee were then incorporated in the bill, which was put up to the Commons for a third reading. If it passed the Houses of Commons and Lords, the Commissioners, who had been named in the bill, then visited the area to be enclosed to see that the provisions of the enclosure were properly carried out and to award compensation to the dispossessed. Their findings had the force of law.

Between 1765 and 1785 there were an average of forty-seven private bills every year; by these means the new methods of farming, advocated by agricultural reformers like Townshend, Coke and Bakewell, were able to be translated into meaningful agricultural advances. The pace of enclosures continued to quicken into the nineteenth century; by 1837, when Victoria came to the throne, the enclosure of open fields was complete, but the enclosing of common land was to go on until about 1870. Indeed the movement gained such momentum that between 1845 and 1870, when it virtually came to an end, no fewer than six hundred thousand acres were enclosed by private acts of Parliament.

As it is now more than a century since the enclosure movement came to an end, it should be possible to take a detached view and to draw up a balance sheet of profit and loss. It is not enough just to say that the profits went to the 'haves' and the losses to the 'have-nots', because society as a whole did derive benefits in the eighteenth and nineteenth centuries from enclosures. Without them there would have been starvation. All the same, while praising the economically admirable consequences of rationalising our agriculture, which enclosure made feasible, it must also be stressed that a great many suffered heavily in the changes brought about in the social structure. The number of the landless greatly increased; they either became underpaid farm labourers or were caught up in the new servitude of unregulated factories. In a parliamentary democracy grievances may be righted by the ballot box, but unfortunately there is often a tragic time-lag. The dispossessed farmers who had become factory workers had to wait until 1867 to get the vote, while those who stayed on the land as farm labourers had to wait even longer, until 1884.

The Fool — a feature of all medieval fairs

Fairs in the Middle Ages

Mention of a fair today conjures up the sights and sounds of a noisy, brightly-lit place of entertainment, whose mechanical amusements bring excitement to the young and dismay perhaps to their elders, especially if they live near the field where the fair is held several times a year. Modern fairs of this kind however have only developed in this way in the last two hundred years, before which time entertainment of a sort, though a feature of earlier fairs, where they provided relaxation for the merchants, after a busy day of buying and selling, played only a minor, subsidiary role. In the Middle Ages fairs were an essential part of the economic life of the country, whose social significance in the course of time came to equal even their economic importance. Such fairs were essential to the development of trade between towns, between districts and indeed sometimes between countries at a time when there was little mobility and chances of meeting people from outside were few and far between.

To understand the need for such opportunities to facilitate trade between one locality and another, readers will have to take a long backward look to a time when needs could only be satisfied by exchanging goods with neighbours, who would not only have to have a surplus of the goods required but also themselves wanted to acquire their neighbour's surplus. The early history of the eastern Mediterranean provides an excellent example of this sort of barter. Phoenician traders, living in Tyre and Sidon, sailed to Greek waters where they were able to exchange their surplus ivory and gold for certain precious shells, only obtainable in Greek waters, from which murex shells the Phoenicians extracted a purple dye, with which they dyed their cloth. Thereafter on visits to far-off Cornwall they exchanged their purple cloth for the much-desired local product, tin. Meanwhile the people of Athens took full advantage of the ivory and gold in the beautification of the statues in their temples.

As life became more complicated however barter proved less and less successful in supplying human needs and hence a search was made for suitable durable objects of more or less constant value, which were thought to provide acceptable standards of value. An island people might choose a particular shell, while a rural one might choose an animal; in early Roman days a cow came to be accepted as providing such a standard, and in consequence rough pieces of iron, a commodity of which the Romans had a plentiful supply, were crudely stamped with the likeness of a cow. Gradually the bar of iron was reduced to just a circular piece, which bore the imprint of a cow. Thus Rome acquired her first coins, though the credit for being the first to invent coinage must go to the people of Lydia, in Asia Minor, one of whose kings — rather fittingly — became associated with the accumulation of great wealth, Croesus himself!

A thousand years passed; if homo sapiens has learnt anything at all down the ages, a surmise sometimes difficult to sustain, it is that progress is by no means inevitable and automatic. Indeed in the dark years after the break-up of the Western Roman Empire in the 5th century AD, a disaster that was followed by the flooding of Europe by barbarian hordes from Asia, mankind certainly took a great backward step. Eventually, after a tragic lapse of several centuries, the trend was somehow reversed and man began again to look to the future, thanks in part to the leadership given by the Christian church, but if the Church supplied the leadership, the newly-populated towns and villages provided the social context. Here men and women foregathered and soon felt the urgent need again to buy and sell. This then was the background to life in the early Middle Ages in which markets began to gather strength.

Here a note of caution has to be sounded as a clear distinction needs to be drawn between local markets, which arose spontaneously out of local needs, and fairs, which in the early years of their development were associated with the Church, which, along with the churchyard at the local level comprised a community centre in a secular sense in the Middle Ages. The priest would encourage his parishoners to attend church not only on Sundays but also on special occasions, such as saints' and patronal days. After such religious observances the worshippers were encouraged to adjourn to the churchyard, where their other needs were attended to. There, in the northern part of the churchyard, which throughout the Middle Ages remained unconsecrated, food and drink were on offer and recreational facilities provided, of which the most popular was dancing. Not surprisingly in the course of time there also gathered in the churchyard traders and pedlars, who saw their chance and took it with both hands.

Such a pattern of development is likely to have been widespread in Western Europe in the early part of the Middle Ages; in this country, as small fairs flourished, the King's interest was gradually aroused and, as supreme ruler of the land, he assumed the right to authorise and to regulate these fairs, which he proceeded to do by the granting of charters to local landowners, most of whom will probably have been officials of the Church, whose secular power was thereby considerably increased. This royal interest in the fairs accelerated in the 13th century, King John, who reigned from 1199 to 1216, granting 117 charters for fairs, while his son, Henry III granted more than 500.

Such a charter spelt out clearly when and where these fairs were to be held, how long they should last, naming the dates every year when they were to be held. In addition tolls to be paid by stall-holders were stated and all other financial aspects of conducting a fair made clear. The most important fair in England, and indeed one of the four great fairs of Europe, was St Bartholomew's in London; the royal charter was granted to the Prior of St Bartholomew's to whom all the profits were originally given, but later when the fair spread and overlapped the existing market at Smithfield, a reassessment of the financial arrangements became necessary, as a result of which the Prior had to share his profits with the City of London, who represented the interests of Smithfield Market.

Even though markets and fairs were alike devoted to the same everyday task of buying and selling, a clear distinction must be made between them, as fairs were to markets what, in the world of football, international matches are to local derbies! Some fairs were of quite short duration, perhaps of two or three days, while others lasted several weeks, but one and all became very important indeed because most of the trade in the Middle Ages was transacted there; in this country alone there were nearly five thousand fairs, some of which were regularly attended by merchants from far-off parts, though at first foreign traders, and indeed sometimes even traders from other parts of this country, were discouraged until the King stepped in and decreed that all traders, be they from near or far, should be made welcome at the fairs. Thereafter many a fair in England had displayed prominently in a central position, often on the outside of the parish church, either a wooden hand or a large, stuffed glove, which intimated to all strangers that they would be most welcome in the area for the duration of the fair. The commercial importance of fairs can hardly be exaggerated but their non-commercial aspects too need to be given their proper, considerable due.

The dominance of the Church in the lives of ordinary people in the Middle Ages ensured that many fairs were sited in places of special religious significance, such as near a monastery, or in a town which possessed a cathedral or a parish church to which pilgrimages were sometimes made. Sites of three such fairs come immediately to mind, those at St Bartholomew's in London, at St Giles in Winchester and outside the cathedral in Canterbury. Many pilgrims, visiting these fairs and indeed many others with similar religious associations, travelled great distances and on arrival required accommodation and entertainment, which were made available to them by the organisers of the fairs, who will also have seen to it that their religious interests were adequately catered for.

Local arrangements for the organisation of fairs were thorough and detailed, born of long experience. Normally the site was a field in a central position, though occasionally, when a fair was on a small scale, lasting only a day or two, it took place in the churchyard. Whatever the location, the local magnate, who received the King's charter, be he a cleric or a lord, appointed a Warden of the Fair, an appointment which may have been largely honorary, because he also appointed a Steward, who had the real authority to get things done. This steward next appointed as many helpers (bailiffs) as he felt he needed, their task to prepare the field, set up the tents, recruit carpenters to build the necessary stalls and booths. The tenants of the houses nearest to the site for the fair were required to vacate their homes and find alternative accommodation, thus enabling the steward to arrange for the letting of their houses to visiting merchants, doubtless at inflated prices! A number of watchmen were also enrolled, whose task it would be to arrest those who broke the law and to hand the prisoners over to a specially convened court which dealt with all the problems connected with the running of the fair. On these occasions there was always a fire risk, which made it necessary to have a number of fire-fighters on call, who would see to it that buckets of water were placed at strategic points. Finally clear notices were posted in public places, notifying all and sundry of the financial arrangements for the fair; all tolls and taxes were there clearly stated.

Merchants, as they arrived, were required to report to the steward, whose task it was to allocate to them suitable houses and stalls in the fair. On the day the fair was to begin, a great service was held in the parish church, where a solemn mass was celebrated, after which a colourful procession took the assembled company back for the official opening of the fair. As the various stalls began to trade, all shops in the locality were expected to close, and to remain closed until the fair was disbanded.

Readers are reminded that the naves of parish churches were not consecrated before the Reformation in the sixteenth century; they were all-purpose meeting places, which were used for worship on Sundays and for secular gatherings in the week. Medieval priests, remembering that most of their Sunday congregations were unable to read, saw to it that the interior walls of the nave were decorated with coloured pictures of people and events, portrayed in the Bible. On weekdays, especially in fair time, people, both parishoners and visitors, thronged the naves to watch the presentation of religious dramas enacted there. Some of the most popular dramatic entertainments provided in the fairs were the so-called Mystery plays, a general name given to simple dramas, based on Bible stories and especially on the birth, life, passion and death of Christ. Temporary scaffolding was built in the nave for these performances, whose actors were mostly priests, though occasionally suitable lay people were allowed to take minor parts. During fair times the bigger towns had in addition movable stages to which the Mystery plays were transferred after being performed in the naves. Frequently this movable waggon gave other performances in the churchyard, before moving to the middle of the fair.

In addition to these dramatic performances, other attractions of a more mundane and down-to-earth nature were organised for the relaxation of merchants and other visitors. Pride of place naturally went to the central booths where food and drink were obtainable, around which there tended to congregate peripatetic entertainers, jugglers, jesters, clowns, stilt-walkers, and frequently puppet-masters, whose raucous tableaux suggested the ever-popular Punch and Judy shows of later years. All was noise and bustle, clamour and colour, combining to create a friendly atmosphere in which visitors and local residents became acquainted with each other and in the process interchanged ideas. All this took place, be it remembered, at a time when, apart from these infrequent fairs, there was widespread social isolation. At the fairs every way was explored whereby the needs of the visitors could be satisfied; stalls were set up at convenient places where money changers were prepared to make local currency readily available. The ultimate in anticipating the wishes of those attending the fair was achieved in those towns (and there were a number of them) in whose parish churches priests stood ready to marry any strangers who desired to take advantage of this unexpected opportunity.

Such were medieval fairs, one of the great institutions of the Middle Ages, when people were more aware perhaps than we are today of the obligations and responsibilities of living in a community.

Social life in the churchyard (Craswall church, Herefordshire) —
note the stone seating around the walls.

Social Life in the Churchyard

In the Middle Ages the parish was a much more self-contained community than it is today. The local land-owner as lord of the manor appointed the priest, who every Easter called a meeting of the parishoners at which two men were elected for a year to act as church wardens, one of these to act as the priest's warden while the other was to further the interests of the people. This latter, the people's warden became the key figure in the secular life of the parish. Another appointment at the same Easter meeting was of a village constable, who had thereafter to take his orders from the wardens. As things worked out, the people's warden became no less than the Warden of the Community Centre, for that is what the church and the churchyard amounted to in a social sense.

The churchwarden's power base was the Church House, which was normally situated in the northern, unconsecrated side of the churchyard, where the accounts were kept and where the warden's band of helpers arranged all the many secular activities that went on in the churchyard or, if the weather was unfavourable, were transferred to the nave of the church, also unconsecrated in the Middle Ages, which served as an all-purpose meeting hall. When it is remembered that the church authorities only made themselves responsible for the maintenance and upkeep of the chancel, the porch and the south side of the churchyard, it will be realised how very onerous were the duties of the churchwarden in having to find ways and means of acquiring enough money to maintain the nave, as well as the north side of the churchyard, especially as there were no other sources of revenue available at that time, other than, in an emergency, recourse to taking the hat round. The wonder is that Easter after Easter there were volunteers, prepared to come forward to undertake such responsible duties on which the welfare and the well-being of the whole parish depended.

Before proceeding further with churchyard activities, organised by the churchwarden, readers' attention must first be drawn to an ancient right granted in the early days of the Christian church to those who had fallen foul of their fellows, the right to seek sanctuary on holy ground. In 399 the Church recognised the right of sanctuary in church, extending the right to the churchyard in 431. The first reference to this right here came in 600, when Ethelbert, King of Kent, confirmed the right of Sanctuary, which was thereafter available not only to those who had broken the law, but also to those who were themselves the victims of criminal activity. Occasionally such victims were granted the additional temporary privilege of storing their worldly goods in the churchyard.

Down to 1066 the right of sanctuary was limited to nine days but in 1070 William I extended the privilege to forty days but insisted that if the refugee had not by the end of that time come to an understanding with his persecutor, he would have to appear, clad in sackcloth, before the Coroner in the church porch, where he would have to "abjure the realm", that is, to swear on oath that he would leave the country within forty days, for which journey a safe passage was guaranteed, but with a less than generous time allowance. The pattern of sanctuary was slightly different in Wales, where the boundary of sanctuary was, according to the Book of Llandaf, "between the yew tree (at the gate) and the church door". Giraldus Cambrensis, writing a few years later, said, "The churches in Wales are more quiet and tranquil than those elsewhere. Around them the cattle graze peacefully, not only in the churchyard but outside too, within the fences and ditches marked out and set by bishops to fix the sanctuary limits."

The use of churchyards as a refuge declined with the passing of the Middle Ages, as thereafter much harsher penalties became increasingly imposed. First Henry VIII in 1529 caused those who abjured the realm to have the back of their right thumb branded by the Coroner with an A, and in 1540 the right was abolished altogether for those charged with rape, murder and burglary. In 1623 James I virtually abolished it, although occasionally well into the nineteenth century sanctuary was granted to those in debt.

In the Middle Ages the parish church was the very centre of village life — the priest saw to that on Sunday, but the church was equally busy in the week, especially if the weather was bad, causing the villagers to meet their friends in the porch or nave, instead of in the churchyard, the normal village social centre. All will have been very familiar with the heavy presence of the dark yew trees, which were a special feature on the south side. When in earlier times the seekers after sanctuary were allowed to bring their goods into the churchyard to be safe, it was to the yews that they looked to provide the necessary protection. In later years the number of yews greatly increased as the result of an order made by Edward I, who in 1307 decreed that all church authorities should plant avenues of yews to protect the porch and entrance of the church from high winds and storms. Worshippers were also made aware of the importance of yews in preparing for the celebration of Easter; on Ash Wednesday the faithful smeared their foreheads with the ash from yew, while on Palm Sunday the procession around the churchyard in which hazel catkins usually deputised for palms, very often, if the season was late, had to make do with boughs of yew.

The tedium of village life was periodically relieved by the traditional observance of festivals, not all of which involved activity in the churchyard, although certainly in at least two of them the churchyard played a central role, at Easter and at Whitsun. On Palm Sunday, when the triumphant entry of Christ into Jerusalem was remembered, the congregation in church, led by the priest and choir, left the church through the north door and went in procession around the churchyard in a clockwise direction, or as people at that time would have said, sunwise, re-entering the church through the porch and the south door. In addition either on Palm Sunday or on the following Saturday evening, all the graves were decorated, either with hazel sprigs or yew and bunches of Spring flowers.

At Whitsun, celebrations were less muted and more boisterous with the churchwarden having to bring out the maypole from storage in the Church house before having it erected in the middle of the north side of the churchyard, around which much dancing then took place, followed by considerable eating and drinking.

On All Hallow E'en, the last day of October, the churchyard was again very busy, though what went on there that night was dictated more by necessity than by any religious sense. As the Middle Ages wore on, in most churchyards there was a serious problem of overcrowding. Year after year on All Hallow E'en bones from former graves, which had a year previously been dug up and stored in a charnel house in the churchyard, were taken out and consumed in a great parish bonfire, as a prelude to replacing them in the charnel house with more bones from the older, overcrowded graves. This great fire of bones, which was originally known as a bone-fire, became very popular indeed, partly because, it was fondly believed, that the flames helped to drive off the evil spirits which were thought to throng the night air at that time of year.

Every church had its own patronal day, a time of special rejoicing, when parishoners commemorated either the dedication of the church or the birthday of the saint to whom the church was dedicated. Great was the rejoicing; first of all there was an evening service in the church, preceded by a candle-lit procession, to be followed the next day by a public holiday, when the north side of the churchyard became the centre of much junketing and jubilation. Grown-ups, as well as children, participated in the various diversions, in dancing and in playing games, and in general merry-making. For many this was the most enjoyable day of the year, but, not surprisingly, in the course of time the festival became debased and rightly subject to much criticism, until authority stepped in and stopped these wakes.

Very much more knowledge of churchyard activities after the Reformation is available because of the large number of churchwardens' accounts that have survived, to be found today in the safe custody of record offices. From these invaluable aids to the study of local history it can be seen that churchwardens were more or less involved in every aspect of parish life. Before government in later centuries began to make it its business to help the sick and the needy, churchwardens did their utmost to identify with most of the problems that beset parishoners, but, as always, solutions to such problems largely depended on the supply of money available. To return to the churchyard during the sixteenth, seventeenth and eighteenth centuries the wardens, in an admirable attempt to raise money, organised parish ales there, despite many threats from London and elsewhere to curb their activities.

When a local need arose, maybe to help a family that had fallen on hard times, or perhaps to swell the meagre dowry of an impoverished bride, a warden would approach local farmers with a request to let him have as much malt as could be spared, which he then took to the Church house where as much strong ale as possible was brewed. Once the ale was ready and once a suitable supply of food had been cajoled from better-off parishoners, a day was fixed for the church ale to take place in the churchyard. Those who participated in the quaffing of ale and the consumption of the food, were expected to pay according to a fixed tariff, which in most parishes saw to it that bachelors paid more than married men, and visitors more than local parishoners.

Henry VIII did what he could in the sixteenth century to stop these ales, in an edict which proclaimed that an end should be put to all eating and drinking in church and churchyard. Despite this edict and other such threats from above, the practice was still popular in many areas at the end of the seventeenth century. In the next century however there was growing evidence that many of these ales had lost their earlier motivation to help others and were becoming little more than excuses for drunken sprees. "By the nineteenth century," comments Christina Hole, "with only a few exceptions the whole custom was gone and was no more than a fading memory."

Last but by no means the least popular of the activities in the churchyard were the games, in which both young and old took part; the north side, which after all had long been recognised as the village playground, witnessed a great variety of games, including wrestling, football, marbles, throwing the hammer and above all fives. Most of these activities were acceptable to the church authorities, except when they coincided with the hours of divine service. Fives seem to have been the most popular pastime, judging by the number of references to it in churchwardens' accounts and elsewhere; its popularity can probably be explained by the excellent facilities for the game provided by church walls and buttresses. Again and again wardens referred to the extra expenditure incurred in replacing broken windows! So very popular did fives become that in some churchyards, especially in Wales, seating accommodation had to be provided for spectators. Parson Woodforde, in his eighteenth century diary, mentioned in a July entry, from Somerset, "We all spent the greatest part of the afternoon in the churchyard, playing at fives against the church wall, I fear, . . . I won a betting of £0.2.9." On many church walls on the north side may still be seen iron hinges, from which in former times hung wooden shutters, which helped to protect the glass. In some areas, especially in north Wales, the playing of fives was encouraged on Sunday afternoons, while in two churchyards in the Golden Valley of Herefordshire, at Newton St Margaret's and at Craswall the playing of fives is confirmed not only by references in the wardens' accounts but also by the survival of visual evidence of stone slabs, clamped to the north wall, where seemingly they acted as score-boards.

There was another very popular activity in the churchyard which could not be classified today as a game but rather as a blood-sport, namely cock-fighting. From Tudor times this sport became very popular and by the seventeenth century cockfighting mains took place in very many churchyards, and even occasionally in the naves of churches, when the weather interfered. In the churchyard at Craswall, just referred to, the clear outline of a cock-fighting arena can still be seen in the long grass. Cockfighting was finally driven out of church and churchyard by an act of Parliament in 1849.

To finish this chapter on a less discordant note, a brief mention must be made of probably the most widely-practised of all churchyard activities, when the weather allowed, dancing. From the early years of the Middle Ages down almost to the end of the nineteenth century, dancing of one kind or another accompanied a variety of churchyard celebrations, including fairs, patronal festivals, weddings and church ales. Dancing in the churchyard lasted longer in Wales, seemingly a pleasure-loving country until it succumbed to non-conformist public opinion. Churchyards today have been rescued from all secular activity, the noisy pastimes and the happy dancing have all gone. Peace has returned, the peace of a deserted place, where the grass grows long and nature has resumed her sway.

A Banker
*The banker, quill in hand, is writing up his accounts
at the end of a day's trading.*

Usury and Banking

According to the dictionary a usurer is one who takes interest on a loan; such a person today would be the bank manager who authorises a loan to the customer, or the building society manager who arranges a mortgage for the would-be house buyer. No-one today grumbles at such activities; on the contrary, they are universally welcomed, even though the actual rate of interest may sometimes seem alarmingly high. Yet there was a time when the law of the land regarded usury, i.e. the charging of interest, as a crime and the Church forbade the practice absolutely to all Christians. Indeed usurers who failed to repent in time were refused Christian burial, sometimes even their wills being annulled.

In even earlier times all trade consisted of exchanging goods for goods; this system of barter satisfied most human needs for many a century and gave rise to the existence of markets where, as commercial life became more complicated, it became desirable to relate goods on offer to an acceptable standard. Eventually, after many experiments with standards such as shells, sheep and cows, a metallic standard was agreed upon because of the durable quality of iron and bronze, which were the first metals to be used for this purpose. The advantage of coins soon became obvious and the possession of money greatly aided the expansion of all commercial activity. However, seeing that in former days when a man had lent his fellow an axe, he had not expected to make any profit on the loan, so now society frowned heavily upon the man who, having lent some coins to another, looked to receive extra coins in return, when the debt was paid. Money was considered dead and sterile and no-one had the right, it was believed, to expect any return from lending it. Such a course of action was thought morally indefensible since whoever gained from it was merely taking advantage of the misfortunes of another.

When industry and agriculture began to expand on a large scale in the later middle ages in England, large sums of money were required but the law still refused to sanction the charging of any interest at all. Not even governments, however, can for ever fly in the face of economic facts; as the need for capital grew, so interest was charged, unofficially and often excessively, giving rise to the general connotation of usury. The excessive rates often imposed became inevitable because of the high risk involved in breaking the law, which absolutely prohibited it.

In general, the lending of money on which the expanding industry and commerce of European Christians depended was left to the Jews who, as pariahs of Europe, were hardly expected to live up to the high standards of Christian conduct! The Jews, already unpopular for being descended from forebears who were held responsible for the crucifixion of Christ, now became even more hated, when they turned to the business of money lending which made them rich. It has to be remembered that the Jews had been denied entry to the guilds where their business abilities might have found a legal outlet.

In the twelfth century the services of the Jews were very much in demand. In France, in the reign of Philip Augustus (1180-1223), protected by the king, they were able to exact as much as forty-six per cent on the money they lent, while in this country where the usual rate charged was one penny in the pound each week, a great deal of money was lavished on cathedrals and monasteries as a result of loans negotiated by the church authorities and Jewish money lenders. In the same century Henry II (1154-1189), who understood the economic importance of large loans, protected the Jews from those who would do them harm. However, when Henry died in 1189, the situation changed dramatically. The coronation of his successor, Richard I, was the signal for the outbreak of anti-semitic riots in London and elsewhere in the country, of which the most serious one was in York. Although the rioting eventually died down, the tide of hostility towards the Jews continued to run dangerously high until in 1290, in the reign of Edward I, they were driven out of the country altogether, to the great satisfaction of the majority but to the economic displeasure of those who depended on the Jews for loans. The economic vacuum their expulsion left was soon to be filled by Italians who hailed from the Plain of Lombardy. As for the Jews, they were to stay away from England until invited back in 1650 by the Commonwealth.

The resentment felt towards the Jews was very soon transferred to the men from Lombardy who took over their money-lending functions when the Jews were driven from the English scene. These men from the south were very resourceful in their behaviour in the money market; they were fully aware both of the great need that English businessmen had of their services and also of the firm opposition these same would-be clients manifested towards paying any interest on money borrowed. Their sharp Italian wits stood them in good stead; they proceeded to lend their money without charging any interest but, if the debtor showed the slightest delay in repaying a loan, he had to pay heavily for the privilege. Such delays were of course inevitable and indeed the extra money charged was generally paid without a murmur, even by those who had hitherto condemned the charging of interest as morally intolerable!

The Lombards gave their name to the area in London where they conducted their affairs; here they sat on benches in Lombard Street doing business with all and sundry who required loans. Items of value such as jewels were required by the lenders by way of security for the loans they made, for which receipts were given to the borrowers. The tendency thereafter grew for those receipts to acquire the value of the loans against which the valuables had been taken as security, and to be accepted as such for currency purposes, thus constituting an early form of paper currency. At about the same time, similar receipts, given by goldsmiths and silversmiths to customers who lodged valuables with them for safe keeping, likewise acquired an acceptable monetary value.

Lombard Street will occasionally have witnessed unpleasant incidents when clients of the Italian bankers, wrathful perhaps at being required to pay more than was deemed fair for overdue payment of loans, kicked over the benches on which the unfortunate men sat and broke them. 'Bankrupt', etymologically, means 'broken bench', its meaning clear in this context! Further evidence of the Lombardian influence may even today still be seen on a bank note, on the front of which, no matter what the denomination, are printed the words 'LONDON FOR THE GOV^R AND COMP^A OF THE BANK OF ENGLAND', Comp^A being an abbreviation of Compagna, the Italian word for Company.

As the banking reputation of gold and silversmiths spread and the Lombards and their English imitators widened the scope of their moneylending activities, the dividing lines between them became so narrow that to many the differences became imperceptible. Less is heard from then on of the Lombards and more of their English counterparts, though the former still seem, well after the middle ages had ended, to have gravitated towards those with money, like bees smelling out pollen. Joseph Strutt, writing in 1800 in THE SPORTS AND PASTIMES OF THE PEOPLE OF ENGLAND, quoted an early sixteenth century author who reported that Henry VIII, when still a young king in the early years of the sixteenth century, became an enthusiastic tennis player "which propensity being perceived by certain crafty persons about him, they brought in Lombards to make wagers with him and so he lost much money".

By the second half of the sixteenth century most people had come to accept the rightness of a reasonable rate of interest being charged, but still Parliament stood out, passing an act in 1552 which quite explicitly forbade the charging of interest, describing it as a "vice most odious and detestable". By 1571 however a sense of reality had at last reached Westminster; in that year the charging of interest was for the first time allowed, providing that it did not exceed ten percent. About the same time there was published a book entitled "Description of England", whose author, William Harrison, wrote "Usury, a trade brought in by the Jews, was now perfectly practised almost by every Christian and so commonly that he is accounted for a fool that doth lend his money for nothing." Just twenty-five years after the law was passed sanctioning a moderate rate of interest, Shakespeare made Shylock in "The Merchant of Venice", say in an aside when being introduced to Antonio, "he lends out money gratis and brings down the rate of usance."

Capitalist ideas gained much ground in the seventeenth century, especially in those countries where the Reformation had taken root; the progress however would have been even faster but for the survival in some quarters of opposition to the very charging of interest at all. In England the law now allowed a moderate rate of interest but it was some time before all sections of society were prepared to accept it. With the restoration of the monarchy in 1660, the necessity for it seems at last to have been realised, as thereafter discussion for the most part centred around the ideal rate to be charged; the low rate current in prosperous Holland was much quoted by its supporters.

Meanwhile, and especially in the second half of the seventeenth century, the goldsmiths became increasingly important as successful merchants looked around to find safe custody for their profits. Their services were offered them by the goldsmiths who, in the reign of Charles II, were prepared to offer six per cent interest to those merchants who would deposit their profits with them. The goldsmiths then lent out on short term loans the money deposited with them and in so doing, came to discharge some of the functions associated in later days with banks. Thus there were bankers in Lombard Street before there were banks there!

The success of banks in Holland prompted much talk in London but the establishment of a bank here was probably delayed by the clear recollection of royal acquisitiveness in Charles I's reign. Pepys' diary contains an entry in August 1666 which discusses the matter. He concluded: "The unsafe condition of a Bank under a monarch makes it hard to have a bank here." Pepys, very much a man of his time, on several occasions referred to going down to Lombard Street, where he borrowed money, some of which he proceeded to lend out to others for short periods; he admitted to his diary that he averaged seven per cent on such deals.

Less than thirty years after Pepys had doubted the wisdom of having a bank in London, the Bank of England came into existence. In 1694 Dutch William, now William III of England, had an expensive war on his hands; in his need to thwart the ambitions of the French king, Louis XIV, he borrowed more than a million pounds from some London goldsmiths. Knowing that wars make no profits and that therefore he would never be able to repay the loan, Wiliam authorised the goldsmiths to issue paper notes to the full value of the loan, at the same time compelling the people of England to accept these notes as legal tender. These same goldsmiths then banded themselves together and became the Bank of England.

Rebecca in Action —
an artist's impression of a ferocious 'female' attack on a toll-gate.

Turnpikes and Tollgates

The roads of this country which the Romans had built were allowed over the centuries to fall into a sorry state of disrepair; in the middle ages most of the trade and commerce of England went by water, taking advantage of river navigations and inshore transport along the coasts. That some roads were maintained at all was due to the patient voluntary work undertaken by the monasteries, whose useful life came to an abrupt end at the hands of Henry VIII in the 1530s. In consequence, Parliament had to turn its attention to the upkeep of the roads. By a series of Highway Acts in 1555, 1562 and 1586 a new system of road maintenance was brought into being, whereby responsibility was delegated by government to every parish in the land, whose job it was to appoint a local Surveyor of Roads, who was to be unpaid. This unfortunate official had then to coerce farmers and landowners in the parish to provide, free of charge, vehicles and materials, and to force parishoners to contribute a certain number of days of labour on the roads every year. This very haphazard system of statute labour was still in force at the beginning of the eighteenth century; at best it was barely adequate, at worst, virtually non-existent.

The rapid commercial and industrial expansion demanded by developments here in the early years of the eighteenth century was seriously impeded by the inefficiency of the existing transport system. Roads and vehicles were both quite inadequate to assume the new burdens about to be imposed upon them. That revolutionary changes were long overdue can be deduced from many sources. Let Macaulay speak for them all: "It was by the highways that both travellers and goods generally passed from place to place. And those highways appear to have been far worse than might have been expected from the degree of wealth and civilization which the nation had even then attained. On the best lines of communication the ruts were deep, the descents were precipitous, and the way often such as it was hardly possible to distinguish, in the dusk, from the uninclosed heath and fen which lay on both sides."

It was not only the roads that were unsuited to the greater needs of the new age but also the vehicles that lumbered over them. A succession of governments had indeed been long aware of the shortcomings of the system of road transport, there having been as early as in 1621 a Royal Proclamation, which had aimed at limiting the size and weight of all vehicles on public roads. Unfortunately this early attempt at necessary regulation had to be called off because of the opposition it provoked. A century later in 1718 Parliament did succeed in limiting the number of horses that were allowed to pull a vehicle; this was followed up in 1741 by an official regulation that there were to be stationed at intervals on certain roads weighing machines to check passing vehicles, with an accompanying tariff of heavy fines to be paid by the drivers of offending vehicles. Parliament again acted in 1753 when it passed the Broad Wheels Act which laid down that nine inches was to be the minimum width of wheels on all vehicles except on light carts and traps. The thinking behind this regulation was that broad wheels would tend to roll a road rather than to cut it up. Meanwhile, the volume of traffic increased enormously as the eighteenth century wore on; not only were many more people wanting to travel, but industry was expanding very quickly indeed and, at the same time, there was a great surge in the amount of trade taking place between the provinces and London.

Statute labour had been found wanting almost from the very beginning; the local surveyors, unpaid as they were, could not be compelled to perform their tasks and, even when they did their best, they had no funds at their disposal to pay for the materials that the adequate maintenance of the roads called for. From time to time those universal providers of solutions to local problems, the Justices of the Peace, did what they could to force parishes to accept their obligations in this respect, but nothing in the circumstances could have made the system work efficiently. Just once there was a glimmer of hope during the short life of the Commonwealth, when statute labour was for a time suspended and there was put in its place a local rate, levied on the wealth of the landowners through whose lands the roads passed. Landowners of course objected so that, when the monarchy was restored, statute labour was brought back too. However in 1662 the newly-restored surveyors were given the power for the first time to levy a rate, if they needed to, to make up for the shortcomings of statute labour. This new power was unfortunately very seldom used.

In 1663 another experiment began which, though short-lived, was later to bring about a much needed improvement in the state of the roads. An Act of Parliament gave to the Justices of the Peace of Hertfordshire, Cambridgeshire and Huntingdonshire the right to set up the first Turnpikes, that is to say, empowered them to build tollgates where users of roads had to pay money for the privilege of using it, the proceeds to go to road maintenance. After the roads in East Anglia were in consequence greatly improved, the turnpikes were removed. Nevertheless the way had been shown and the principle had been adopted that those who used the roads should pay for their upkeep.

In the next forty years there were several more similar acts, which lasted for short periods; in every case Justices of the Peace were made the agents for setting up and organising the toll gates and toll houses. Then in 1706 Parliament created the first Turnpike Trust, each subsequent trust requiring a separate private act of parliament, which would set up a body of comissioners who then proceeded to erect toll gates, where tolls were exacted on a fixed scale. These Turnpike Trusts soon increased in number but only on the main roads; on all other highways, maintenance still depended entirely on statute labour. Despite this undoubted improvement in those roads maintained by the money provided by the toll gates, the Turnpike Trusts were so unpopular that particularly between 1735 and 1750 there were a number of serious riots in which toll gates were battered down and the toll houses burned, the Rebecca Riots in Wales in 1743 being perhaps the best known. Rioting gradually died down in the second half of the eighteenth century but up to the 1830s when most turnpikes ceased to exist, they had failed to win the support of the travelling public who benefitted most from the improved condition of the roads.

Meanwhile, by Acts of Parliament in 1767 and 1773, the Government tried to make statute labour more efficient on the general highways; this they did by trying to make the burdens fall more equitably on the various parishes concerned. Much was attempted but very little real improvement resulted. At the same time, Parliament also tried with varying degrees of success to improve the efficiency of the Turnpike Trusts by bringing them under the direct control of Justices of the Peace, who thereafter acted as the agents of central government, much in the way they had done before the Turnpike Commissioners had been created in 1706.

So far consideration had been given to the methods of road maintenance — whether the labour and the material required should be provided free of charge under the system of statute labour, or from tolls to be levied on road users by the Turnpike

Commissioners and to the size and type of vehicles allowed upon the roads. When a third and quite different and absolutely essential approach was made to the problems of road transport, namely the actual engineering of the roads, then substantial and lasting improvements in our transport system resulted. Credit for this great achievement belonged above all to three men, John Metcalfe, Thomas Telford and John Loudon McAdam, the first real road engineers.

The Commissioners of the Turnpike Trusts, unlike the organisers of statute labour, having at their disposal the means to pay for skilled advice and assistance, brought into being the new profession of road engineer. The first of this famous trio to be appointed by them was John Metcalfe (1717-1810). 'Blind Jack of Knaresborough' (he lost his sight at the age of six) overcame his handicap sufficiently to fight at Culloden in 1746 and later to drive a stage coach. He turned to roadmaking in the 1760s, when he showed himself to be a pioneer of road drainage. He had ditches dug at the sides of roads into which surplus water could run from the road surface, which he made convex. Blind Jack was also the first engineer to give serious attention to laying firm foundations.

Thomas Telford (1757-1834), after being apprenticed to a stone mason, became Surveyor of Public Works in Shropshire, where he built two famous bridges over the Severn. His first notable achievement as a road engineer was the improvement of the road from Glasgow to Carlisle, before moving south to his greatest work — the making of the road from London to Holyhead, which he started in 1815. Above all, this remarkable engineer, who had in his time made more than a thousand miles of roads and built twelve hundred bridges, was outstanding for the really strong foundations on which he always insisted and on easy gradients.

John Loudon McAdam (1756-1836), an exact contemporary of his fellow Scot — Telford, took up road making rather late in his career, beginning in the south of Scotland in 1810. In 1816 he was appointed Surveyor to the Bristol Turnpike Trust where his roads won such favourable comment that in 1827 he moved to London where he was made Surveyor-General of Metropolitan roads. In that capacity he not only remade existing roads, but also consolidated all the turnpike roads in that area into a unified system. His greatest achievement, as his name suggests, was to concentrate on getting a good surface which would resist wear and tear and which could easily be drained. Furthermore his roads were cheaper to make than Telford's and easier and cheaper to maintain.

Between 1760 and 1774, four hundred and fifty-two Turnpike Acts were passed and by 1800 there were one thousand, six hundred turnpike roads, while by 1835, when the very important Highway Act became law, there were twenty-two thousand miles of turnpiked roads. As the mileage of the roads increased, so did the volume of traffic, while the time taken for most journeys was very much reduced; for instance, between 1754 and 1784 the travelling time of a coach from London to Manchester was halved, from four days to two, and by the time of Waterloo there were no fewer than two hundred carriers operating between the two cities.

Another circumstances, which speeded up the search for better roads and better conveyances, was the development of the post. Most towns in the eighteenth century had a postmaster, whose main duty was to provide a supply of horses at convenient intervals along the roads for the convenience of the travellers who carried the post. Until the middle of the century, letters were carried on horseback but after about 1750, mails began to be conveyed in public coaches, until in 1784, John Palmer of Reading won a contract from the Post Office in London to carry the mail in the new Mail Coaches which very soon became the most popular and the quickest form of transport for ordinary members of the public.

Carefully constructed and properly maintained roads, along with better-designed coaches that provided greater comfort, speed and security for their passengers, together brought a rapid improvement in our system of road transport, which reached its heyday in the early years of the nineteenth century, when by one of history's ironies, it had to face the unequal competition offered by the development of the railways.

The maintenance of the roads was finally regulated by the Highway Act of 1835, whereby they became the responsibility of local Surveyors, whose work was thereafter financed by rates levied on local landowners. This act ended once and for all the system of statute labour, authorising in its stead, local rates for the maintenance of the highway. The roads of this country were thus made ready for the use and enjoyment of the rapidly growing population, but as the population chose instead to travel by train, the roads had to wait a hundred years for the next and terrible challenge, that to be afforded by the internal combustion engine.

An 18th century print of a Justice of the Peace, dispensing justice to poachers, evidence of whose crime may be seen in the fore-ground.

Justices of the Peace

For more than six hundred years the voluntary principle in English life has been continuously and splendidly enshrined in the activities of the Justices of the Peace. From the fourteenth century, when these unpaid but invaluable servants of the crown first received their name, until the passage of the Local Government Act of 1888, which made an end of all their powers except for their judicial responsibilities, they carried upon their broad shoulders a great deal of the burden of the local government of England.

Today Justices of the Peace are appointed by the Lord Chancellor, acting upon the recommendations of the lord-lieutenants of the various counties; they are usually laymen and, as always through their long history, they remain unpaid. They may not be appointed after their sixtieth birthdays, and all must retire at 70. The office is open to both sexes, to all sections of the community, rich and poor, regardless of race and religion and of any and every political persuasion. The appointment is however subject to a residential qualification. The chief remaining duty of JPs today is a very important one, since it is in the magistrate's court, where they preside, that all criminal proceedings begin.

As the population grew in the middle ages and with it the need for more laws and statutes, the King had to depend more and more upon local officials to see that the law of the land was carried out and that reasonable government was maintained at the local level. Much of the responsibility for local government in the past had devolved upon sheriffs, whose office dated back to Anglo-Saxon times; however this early experiment in delegation of power from the central to the local authority seems to have fallen far short of what was required, very largely through the widespread abuse of power by many sheriffs. By the fourteenth century their very name had become a byword for extortion and corruption. In the previous century there had developed another experiment whereby the local gentry, many of whom already represented their counties in parliament, played the role of unpaid local government officials, acting quite independently of the sheriffs, whom they were soon to supplant. In the next century, the fourteenth, Edward III deliberately chose to increase the powers of these unpaid agents of government, the county squires; they were called Keepers or Justices of the Peace and were regarded as the nominees of the King to govern the areas where they lived. In every county in the country by the end of the fourteenth century, JPs had taken over from the sheriffs and were, so to speak, local viceroys. Their chief sphere of influence was in the Quarter Sessions, which came into being in 1362; the name of the court derived from a statute which required that "justices shall keep their sessions in every quarter of the year at least". Quarter sessions became in time the governing body of the counties, where all judicial, executive and administrative decisions were taken. JPs thereafter gradually came to enjoy an enormous range of powers; they were local policemen, judges and civil servants. They arrested wrongdoers, they punished them if they were found guilty, they fixed maximum wages for the locality and decided what prices were fair. Indeed their role became that of supervisors of the entire administration of the counties.

In the sixteenth century the power of JPs was greatly increased and consolidated; in the words of G.M. Trevelyan "they were Elizabeth's maids of all work". The Privy Council in London, which was the real seat of governmental authority in Tudor times, was the apex of political control, from which power devolved to local JPs who were held responsible by the Privy Council for the conscientious execution of their manifold duties. Above all, JPs in Elizabeth's reign were all-important as local agents of government, as authority attempted to wrestle with the acute social and economic problems which the regime had inherited. Poverty was rife, social injustices was widespread and unemployment had assumed quite unacceptable proportions. There was an overriding need for a new radical social policy and when this was forthcoming, the JPs were at hand to see that it was efficiently and justly carried out.

One example must suffice to show how vital was the contribution made by the JPs. In 1563 Parliament, in an effort to bring order out of chaos, passed the Statute of Artificers, which attempted very necessarily to regulate the conditions of employment in every industry. Basically the act demanded that men had to work as agricultural labourers unless they could prove that they were qualified to work at a craft. All work contracts had to run for at least one year and a man was legally entitled to a reference when he left his place of employment. All craftsmen had to serve a seven year apprenticeship. So much for the Statute; its enforcement depended entirely on the industry of the JPs, who in carrying out their duties had to satisfy the ever-watchful eye of the Privy Council. In view of the magnitude of their responsibilities it is indeed surprising that this new system of social change seems to have worked reasonably well and for so many years.

Hand in hand with the local administration of the Statute of Artificers went two other duties, the fixing of rates of pay for all the workers in the locality, such rates having first to pass the scrutiny of the Privy Council before being applied, and the relief of poverty. In this connection local poor rates were first levied in 1572, when JPs were empowered to decide the amount every householder should contribute; in all these duties the JPs were assisted by overseers of the poor.

In the sixteenth century it is certainly no exaggeration to say that the influence of JPs was greater than that of any other group of men in the entire country. They provided a free but efficient local government service, they acted as judges in dealing with local crime and they were held responsible by the Privy Council for such maintenance of roads and bridges as was possible. In addition, they were the right-hand men of government in dealing locally with wages and prices and they had the added task of enforcing the Poor Law. England was better served by her JPs at this time than in any earlier or later century.

Early on in the seventeenth century the special relationship that existed between the Privy Council and the JPs was put under severe strain in the struggle that was brewing between King and Parliament, which was to have a fundamental effect on the history of the seventeenth century. As the quarrel deepened in the course of the century its effect, in this one context, was to lessen the position of supreme authority previously enjoyed by the Privy Council vis-à-vis the JPs. It is obvious that in the unsettled middle years of the century, both during and after the Civil War, normal channels of communication between central and local government depended more on the personal qualities of local JPs than on instructions received from London. In the Restoration the position changed, as Charles II after 1660 virtually allied himself with the Tory Party and the Church of England in opposition to the Whigs and the Dissenters; with the pendulum swinging back in this fashion there was a growing tendency for the Tory Privy Council to send out edicts to the JPs, which many of them were only too happy to carry out, especially where, as often happened, their actions received strong vocal approval from anti-Whig parsons in the pulpits of their parish churches.

Quite early on in Restoration, the youthful Pepys was made a JP;

an entry in the diary for 24 September 1660, when the diarist was only 27 years old, announced the fact: " . . . Sworn justice of the peace for Middlesex, Essex, Kent and Southampton, with which honour I find myself mightily pleased, though I am wholly ignorant in the duties of a justice of the peace . . . " He was soon to find out because in December of the same year, while on an official visit to Woolwich as an Admiralty clerk, a naval captain complained to him that money had been taken from the cabin on his ship. Pepys commented thus: "I did the first office of a Justice of the Peace, to examine a seaman thereupon, but could find no reason to commit him . . . "

In the revolution settlement which followed the abdication of James II in 1688, the government of the country virtually passed into the hands of Parliament; never again thereafter was the King able through his Privy Council to exercise any firm control over local JPs, who accordingly went their own ways, almost untrammelled by restraints from central government. At the end of the seventeenth century there was much more liberty for JPs, who could do more or less as they pleased, which in many cases amounted to very little indeed. Such essential matters as the fixing of wages and the regulation of apprenticeships were frequently forgotten in the pursuit of pleasanter social duties, while the management of the Poor Law was more and more left in the hands of the parish overseers. By the beginning of the eighteenth century JPs were a law unto themselves.

In this eighteenth century heyday of JPs, the parish in England for the last time operated successfully as a political and social unit; once a year at the Easter vestry meeting the parishoners elected their officers, churchwardens, constables and overseers of the poor. In overall control were the JPs, who were generally local land-owners, but as the century wore on, their ranks were sometimes joined by parish priests who often brought a much-needed extra ration of human understanding to the job. By the middle of the century JPs were beginning to acquire a bad reputation in the novels of writers like Smollett and Fielding. Nevertheless, in general, parishes were still being reasonably well served by their JPs, their faults for the most part stemming from ignorance of the living conditions of the poor rather than from greed or corruption, as often alleged. Most of the JPs probably did their best, however inadequate that may have been in the face of changing conditions towards the end of the century, when rural wages were badly lagging behind and were in urgent need of immediate upgrading.

Things came to a head in 1795, by which time the two-year old war with France had already sent prices up, while labourers' wages remained depressed. In May Berkshire JPs met at Speenhamland, a parish near Newbury, in order to deal with the problems that beset agricultural labourers in their parish. Common sense suggested that they should fix a minimum wage which should thereafter be regulated in accordance with the rising price of bread. The magistrates, however, fearful of upsetting the farmers, who would have had to meet the higher wages bill, chose another course of action. They drew up what became known as the Speenhamland Bread Scales. In future a working labourer in need would receive from the parish a sum of money in addition to the basic wage he received from his employer, this extra sum to be geared to the price of a loaf of bread and the size of his family. As bread prices rose, so would the Speenhamland dole. Most other JPs throughout the Midlands and the South of England imitated the Speenhamland Magistrates so that what was virtually parish relief became the normal method of enabling impoverished labourers to make ends meet. Their actual wages stayed as they were. This Speenhamland decision to supplement wages out of rates may have helped to keep starvation at bay but it was morally indefensible and psychologically damaging. It was to stay in force until 1834, when a new poor law was passed by Parliament.

In the bleak years that followed the coming of peace in 1815, acute social, political and economic problems proliferated. Prices soared, wages stayed low, disease spread in the unregulated new towns that mushroomed in the north. In fact thoughts of revolution were in the air. In this raw new world there was no longer any place for the country gentlemen to meet in Quarter

Sessions and take important decisions. It was time for Parliament to act; in 1832 the franchise was at last widened with the middle class getting the vote. New legislation followed, though one of the earliest of its Acts, the Poor Law of 1834, which ended the Speenhamland Bread Scales, was one of its unhappiest achievements. In 1867 the vote was given to workers in the towns, with agricultural labourers having to wait another seventeen years to catch up with them. It is significant that on the very first occasion when farm labourers had the chance to use the vote, at the General Election in 1885, most of them defied the country gentlemen of England, from whose ranks JPs had always been chosen, and sent to Westminster the Liberals. Three years later in 1888 Parliament passed a local government act which created county councils, which thereafter became responsible for the administration of all county matters, thus taking away from the JPs all their remaining administrative functions, leaving them only with the judicial powers that they still enjoy today.

The Pales Quaker burial ground at Llandegley in Powys.

The Quakers

Quakers today have come to be associated in the public mind with three things, philanthropy, pacifism and passive resistance. In the 1914 war many of them were sent to prison for their beliefs but in the second war Quakers generally were treated with more consideration when they appeared before tribunals. Certainly few people today question their sincerity or their courage. Their movement, now more than three hundred years old, was really the brain-child of one man, George Fox, but first it is necessary to look briefly at the historical background of the age which produced him.

For a hundred years after the Reformation, which broke with the Church of Rome in England in the reign of Henry VIII, the authority of the new Protestant Church was, if not unchallenged, at least for most of the time more or less accepted by the majority, but in the Commonwealth, which ruled the country in the interregnum between the death of Charles I in 1649 and the restoration of the monarchy in 1660, religious dissidents were quick to take advantage of new opportunities for dissent by breaking away from the Church of England. Amongst their number were such strangely-named groups as the Levellers, the Diggers, the Ranters, the Fifth-Monarchy Men, the Millennarians and the Muggletonians. Of this remarkable company none was more important than the Society of Friends, whose members were called Quakers by their enemies, who mocked them because they said that they quaked with emotion when they were being moved by religious feelings.

The early history of the Quaker movement is very largely the history of this one man, George Fox, who founded the society. Born in Leicestershire in 1624 Fox began to question the validity of the beliefs of the established church when he was but twenty years of age. It was on the summit of Pendle Hill in Lancashire, a place more associated in the public mind with witchcraft that, after experiencing three years of ever-increasing doubts, he had a vision of a better life, which encouraged him to take the plunge. This he did in 1647 (during a time of mounting civil turmoil in England) when he set out to tour England and Wales, preaching, often in the open air, whenever and wherever he could find an audience. The form of Christianity which he preached forbade all creeds and all sacraments; no priest, he maintained, should be allowed to stand between the individual and his God, while men and women had to be treated as absolute equals. The theme of all Quaker preaching was the all-important need for the individual man or woman to make direct personal contact with God, thus by-passing the priesthood. It is perhaps difficult at this distance of time to understand the intensity of the hatred shown to early Quaker preachers like George Fox. Their distinctive simple dress and their equally distinctive and simple way of speaking made them recognisable everywhere; the broad-brimmed hat and the "thee-and-thou" speech set them apart. One of their most influential sympathisers was Margaret Fell, the wife of one of Cromwell's judges; her home, Swarthmore Hall, near Ulverston, became the unofficial headquarters of the movement in its early days. In later years the widowed Margaret was to become the wife of George Fox.

From the very beginning, the Quakers were persistently persecuted, their tormentors being frequently exasperated by their patience and their refusal to make any secret of their activities or to offer any resistance to opposition. They would not hold their meetings in secret, nor would they, when brought into court, swear an oath. And so society rounded on them, at least twenty thousand of their number suffering punishment for their beliefs, of whom four hundred and fifty actually paid with their lives. This frenzied hatred came not only from members of the established church but also, rather more surprisingly, from their fellow nonconformists. Despite it all, or probably because of it, Quakerism was to flourish in these early years of violent persecution.

From 1647 until he died in 1691 George Fox devoted his entire life to preaching the Quaker way except when his missionary tours were interrupted by periods of imprisonment, which were eventually to undermine his health. In all, he spent six years in prison, dividing his time between gaols in Nottingham, Derby, Carlisle, Launceston, Lancaster, Scarborough and Worcester. His methodically-kept journals survive, from which today's reader may get a marvellous glimpse of life in seventeenth century England.

High up in the remote hills of that part of Powys which used to be called Radnorshire there is still in use a Quaker Meeting House which owed its establishment to the personal influence of George Fox. In 1657 Fox preached for three hours to an enthusiastic outdoor congregation on Pen-y-bont Common, which lies between Knighton and Llandrindod Wells. There the seed was sown. In 1673 a local farmer, who had been greatly moved by what Fox had said on that memorable day, left in his will a piece of land which was to be used as a burial ground for Quakers, whose bodies at death at that time were not allowed to be buried in consecrated ground. Next to this early burial ground near Llandegley the Pales

Meeting House was built in 1713; to this day Quakers still gather there for their meetings.

It needs to be stressed that Quakerism drew its converts from all sections of society, from the very poorest and from men and women of wealth and high position. Of the many Quaker missionaries who opted to go abroad to spread their cause, none is better known than William Penn, who in 1681 received in America, in settlement of a debt due to his father, a large tract of land near the river Delaware. Here Penn set up a model Quaker colony, which came to attract many Quaker emigrants to America, who were in time to make Pennsylvania the freest and the most liberal state in the New World.

The early period of torment and persecution lasted until the Revolution settlement that followed the expulsion of James II and the accession of William III in 1688. The Toleration Act of 1689 made life rather less difficult for Quakers and indeed for all other nonconformists, because they were no longer liable to be hauled to court if they failed to attend the services of the Church of England. Nevertheless Quakers were still less than first-class citizens, continuing to suffer civil disabilities through their refusal to toe the line.

Of the Quakers at the end of the seventeenth century G.M. Trevelyan wrote this: "The Puritan pot had boiled over with much heat and fury; when it had cooled and been poured away, this precious sediment was left at the bottom." In the next century religious attitudes generally underwent a change; the excitement and the bigotry and the sectarianism gave place to the increasing coolness and the growing disinterest of the eighteenth century. It is perhaps significant that the Toleration Act of 1689 did nothing to increase the number of dissidents including the Quakers. For the Quakers the eighteenth century seems to have been a time of consolidation, as they settled down to achieve very considerable results in those occupations to which their civil disabilities restricted them. As they continued to refuse to take the oath and could not in all conscience subscribe to the tenets of the Church of England, they found themselves debarred from many professions.

However, by 1730 it had begun to come to the general notice that some Quakers were becoming prosperous businessmen and what is more that they were doing so by methods that were as conspicuously honest as they were successful. In commerce and banking Quakers began to make their mark in the eighteenth century. One of the first Quaker bankers was John Gurney of Norwich, whose son Joseph John, born in 1788, not only followed in his father's footsteps as a successful banker, but also achieved fame as an outstanding philanthropist; his eldest sister Elizabeth Fry, born in 1780, having learned the dreadful facts of prison life at first hand in Newgate, devoted her life, despite the calls of a very large family, to the far from prestigious cause of prison reform.

Another prominent Quaker of the same generation was Edward Pease (1767-1858); he was born in Darlington, himself the son of a woollen manufacturer, whose trade he continued to practise until 1817, when he threw in his lot with George Stephenson. Thereafter he played a leading part in bringing to life the Stockton to Darlington Railway. In addition, he was an active worker in the cause of anti-slavery. Two of his sons, also enthusiastic Quakers, became Members of Parliament, the elder, Joseph, who was to represent South Durham, being the first Quaker to take his seat in the House of Commons.

Many of the men associated with railway development in its early days were Quakers, both as promoters and investors; another Quaker who took an early interest in the railways was a printer and map-maker from Lancashire, George Bradshaw (1801-1853). He had already published a Map of Inland Navigation when in 1839 he turned his attention to bringing out a railway time-table. In that year he produced a very small book "Railway Time-tables", which he followed up in 1841 by publishing a monthly railway guide. Although neither of the two world wars this century interfered with its regular appearance on the railway bookstalls, a dispute in the printing industry in 1946 caused the very first interruption in the monthly sequence in October of that year. Bradshaw, which had for many years marked the months in the Quaker fashion, First Month etc., is happily still a household name.

Even in the days when they were still being debarred from full citizenship, Quakers were in the van, toiling away to secure vital reforms in areas where few people had yet seen the need for any action. In the last twenty years of the eighteenth century on three occasions, Quakers raised the flag of protest. In 1783 the very first petition to Parliament for the abolition of the slave trade was organised and presented by Quakers, who thereafter played a prominent part in bringing about its abolition many years before they themselves were even allowed to enter Parliament. In 1792 a great landmark in the history of mental illness was reached when Quakers set up the Retreat at York, which became a model for sympathetic and kindly treatment, while in 1798 Joseph Lancaster opened a school for the education of the poor, thus taking the first faltering steps in the long Quaker struggle to acquire schools which should be based on religious principles but without any sectarian bias.

In the nineteenth century by which time the Quakers, like other nonconformists, had managed to convince the establishment-minded lawmakers of England of their worth as thinking minorities, the barriers against full citizenship were piecemeal removed. In 1828 by the repeal of the seventeenth century Test Act, Quakers were no longer ineligible for civil appointment through refusing to take the sacraments. Four years later, Parliament in 1832 permitted elected members to take their seats in the Commons by affirmation instead of by taking the oath, should any member prefer; the previously mentioned member for South Durham, Joseph Pease, was the first Quaker who affirmed. Finally in 1871 the drawbridges at Oxford and Cambridge were let down and Quakers were at long last permitted to pass within.

" . . . I may be wrong as to the facts of what occurred at Manchester but if they were what I have seen them stated, I can never repent speaking of them with indignation. When I cease to feel the injuries of others warmly, to detest wanton cruelty, and to feel my soul rise against oppression, I shall think myself unworthy to be your son . . . "

Macaulay was an undergraduate at Cambridge in 1819, when, a month after Peterloo, he received a stern letter of rebuke from his father for expressing in a recent letter his strong sympathy with those who had protested. He replied as above.

Peterloo

"The future," said Confucius "never lies ahead of us, but always comes flying over our heads from behind." It is as well to bear this in mind when considering the remarkable and tragic events that took place at St Peter's Fields in Manchester on 16 August 1819; at this meeting-place, which in after years was to become the building site for Manchester's most prestigious hotel, the Midland, a very large crowd of working men and women, drawn from all over Lancashire, foregathered in order to listen to speeches to be made by Henry, nick-named Orator, Hunt and his fellow Radicals. Before dealing with the dramatic happenings of that day it is essential to know something of the pressures that had compelled ordinary men and women to go to Manchester in such large numbers. For four years, ever since an uneasy peace had brought the French war to an end, social and economic conditions, particularly amongst those who worked in the new factory towns in the north, had deteriorated to such an extent that the voices of dissent had swelled into a loud enough chorus to reach the ears of Parliament, whose members lived in daily dread of a repetition on

English soil of the terrible drama that had been played out in the streets of Paris twenty years and more before.

Hardly had the 19th century started than repression reared its ugly head in this country; in 1800 the government, ever mindful of the revolutionary excesses perpetrated by political clubs in France in the previous decade, passed the Combination Act, which made illegal the formation of all clubs. This act of parliament intentionally and effectually prevented the growth of trade unions. Thirteen years later at a time when the price of bread had reached a record height, Parliament repealed an Elizabethan statute which had empowered Justices of the Peace at quarter sessions to enforce a minimum wage. From that day onward the downtrodden and the impoverished, while forbidden by the Combination Act from joining a trade union in order to give solidarity to the presentation of their grievances, were also refused by law the protection of the safety net afforded by a minimum wage.

In 1815 peace returned to a war-weary country and, as always at the end of a long war, the air was filled with talk of the need for fundamental change. There was a widespread feeling among the thinking minority, represented by the Radical movement, that wholesale changes had to be sought not only in the economic structure of society but also in the legal and social system. The soldiers came back home and were demobilized; many of them tried to find work in the new factory towns of Lancashire, where there was in consequence a general undercutting of wages. The situation was made worse by the refusal of the government to interfere with what were then thought of as the sacred laws of supply and demand, the market forces of that time. Furthermore it was feared that any concession that was made by the government would be interpreted as an ominous sign of weakness. The seriousness of the wages situation in Lancashire is graphically illustrated by the following statistic: in 1814 a Lancashire weaver received sixteen shillings and sixpence a week, whereas in 1818, by which time the cost of living had risen alarmingly, the weaver's weekly wage had slumped to nine shillings.

The poorer a family, the greater its dependence on the price of bread. In 1815 the House of Commons, the majority of whose members were landowners and farmers, passed the Corn Laws, whereby the import of wheat from abroad was prohibited until home grown wheat reached a certain price. The farmers were thus protected but at the expense of the consumers who were exposed to dearer bread prices at a time of rising unemployment and generally deteriorating economic conditions.

Men, when faced with grievances that threaten the material well-being of their families, will always raise their voices in protest; in a well-ordered society suitable means are provided for expressing this dissatisfaction, but in the post-Waterloo England there were no such safety valves. The right to vote was restricted to those prosperous citizens who owned freehold land assessed at a certain annual value. Hence there was a rapid growth in the demand for an expansion of the franchise to enable the working man — and his unemployed brother — to get the vote in order to clamour legally for vital changes in the ordering of society.

The unfranchised and the underprivileged found a champion in William Cobbett, whose weekly paper, the Political Register (priced at 2d in 1816) became the focal point for discontent and was to play a very prominent part in preparing the public mind for the necessity of sweeping changes. Samuel Bamford, a Lancashire weaver, who was present at Peterloo and wrote a vivid account of it in *Passages in the Life of a Radical*, said this of Cobbett: "At this time the writings of William Cobbett suddenly became of great authority; they were read on nearly every cottage hearth in the manufacturing districts." The answer of the Government to this critical situation was more repression. In 1816 Habeas Corpus was suspended; in the following year five thousand men marched from Manchester to London to protest to the House of Commons. These were the so-called Blanketeers who were turned back by the Army and prevented from entering the capital. Some of them were arrested and imprisoned without trial. The bottle was being corked ever more tightly. There was one other factor that rendered a tense situation even more tense, the absence of a police force, so that the maintenance of law and order was the entire responsibility of the Army, as will be seen in Manchester.

This was the background to the momentous meeting called for the 16th of August 1819 in a large open space in the middle of Manchester, whose population had risen steeply from about seventy thousand in 1800 to nearly one hundred and fifty thousand by this time. Between sixty and eighty thousand men, women and children from all parts of Lancashire had heeded the summons to attend the meeting where Henry Hunt was going to pinpoint their grievances. Above all the suspension of Habeas Corpus was to be highlighted along with the need for parliamentary reform and the widening of the franchise.

On the hustings stood Henry Hunt, whom his enemies sneered at as the Orator; he was an outstanding figure, rendered the more conspicuous by the tall white hat that he sported on these public occasions — and which in after years became the emblem of many Radicals. At 46 he was in his prime; he hailed from Wiltshire, where originally he had been a farmer, but early in the new century he had turned his back on the farming community and become a Radical. Before long people were comparing him with Cobbett but whereas Cobbett relied upon the written word, Hunt's reputation was solely based on his known ability to sway a crowd. Hence posterity still applauds Cobbett but tends to think of Hunt as a cantankerous rabble rouser, which as a historical judgement certainly leaves something to be desired.

As the vast crowd assembled, eye witnesses clearly remembered that no-one was armed and that everybody seemed in good spirits and behaved in a responsible manner. The magistrates who, in the absence of a police force, were responsible for maintaining public order, were on edge. They therefore gave the order that mounted units of the Manchester Yeomanry were to move into the crowd with the intention of arresting the speakers as soon as the meeting began. A hundred cavalrymen rode into the crowd, halting about a hundred yards short of the platform. Hunt, realising the turn events were taking, addressed the crowd, urging them to give the soldiers three cheers and to stay firm. The cheers rang out but further action was only thereby postponed for a minute or two. The cavalry then drew their sabres and charged through those members of the crowd who stood between them and the platform. As the speakers were being hustled away, the crowd turned and fled, causing the chief magistrate to lose his nerve and to summon up the 15th Hussars and the Cheshire Yeomanry, which had been held in reserve. Panic then spread as the Hussars and the Cheshire Yeomanry rode up and down. Within a quarter of an hour St Peter's Fields were empty save for the dead and wounded.

On that day of degradation eleven lives were lost and about six hundred people were injured. Hunt, his white hat slashed by a sabre, was carried off to prison; at the subsequent trial he was sentenced to three years' imprisonment. Predictably he bounced back and in 1830 he was elected MP for Preston. In a short parliamentary career he was to draw attention to himself twice, once when he agitated against the Corn Laws and the other time when he presented a petition demanding rights for women.

Public opinion had been deeply shocked by the excesses of Peterloo, despite the official message of congratulation sent by the Prime Minister to the Manchester magistrates. Anger at what had happened crossed party lines and social classes. Trevelyan's comment was: "Whigs in their high country seats and merchants in their cosy parlours were horrified at the callous slaughter of their fellow citizens. It was called Peterloo because it seemed to cancel the debt of the nation's gratitude for Waterloo."

The young Macaulay, then an eighteen year old undergraduate at Cambridge, found himself in hot water for confiding in a letter to his father that he sympathised with the underdogs at Manchester. In a further letter home he wrote: "I may be wrong as to the facts of what occurred in Manchester; but if they be what I have seen them stated, I can never repent speaking of them with indignation. When I cease to feel the injuries of others warmly, to detest wanton cruelty and to feel my soul rise against repression, I shall think myself unworthy to be your son."

Parliament remained unmoved, however, and before the year was out had passed the Six Acts, one of which forbade all public meetings, unless convened by those in authority, while another imposed a tax of fourpence on all newspapers, thus hoping to prevent ordinary men and women from reading Cobbett's *Register*.

The humble turnip that changed the course of history.

The Roots of Empire

It is one of the surprising curiosities of our history that our dislike of eating meat, which had become tainted through being insufficiently salted, played a considerable part in laying the foundations of the British Empire! Such a ridiculously improbable statement demands an immediate and a proper explanation. Way back in the Middle Ages every autumn, when the pastures became inadequate and suitable fodder for cattle was not available, as there was at that time no known winter feed for cattle, there was an almost total slaughter of the herds, with only a very few beasts spared to survive the rigours of winter before renewing the herds in the Spring. The vast numbers of carcasses that resulted from this unavoidable but tragic and uneconomic culling, had to be preserved in salt in order to satisfy the craving for meat of those people who were prosperous enough to pay for it. Salt however was a very precious commodity and in short supply and therefore expensive; hence more often than not by the Spring of the following year eating insufficiently salted meat was frequently a noisome and unpleasant experience, even though the meat was still presumably nutritious.

It was at this juncture that such palates often became placated by the tempting addition of strong spices to mask the taste of the meat; these spices, which became ever more expensive as the demand for them grew, were imported from eastern countries, from East Africa to the Indies, in which places a very large trade developed over the years. It should perhaps be pointed out that the palates of the poor peasants were not similarly affronted by the taste of tainted meat, as the only occasions when they tasted meat was when their palates were whetted by the delights of poached rabbit.

Many of these precious cargoes of spices were carried by Arab and Portuguese ships up the east coast of Africa or across the Indian Ocean and up the Arabian Sea, where they were brought ashore and transferred to the backs of camels for the arduous journey westwards to the ports on the east coast of the Mediterranean; from here these valuable commodities were taken by various routes over land and sea to their eventual markets in northern and western Europe. At the same time the immense and terrifying Turkish thrust from central Asia westwards was gaining an awful momentum, until Constantinople itself fell to the Turks in 1453; from the middle of this fifteenth century, when this long-feared and long-threatened event took place, victorious Turkish soldiers came to control all the overland caravan routes and proceeded to impose heavy taxes on the caravans, as they moved to the west. These taxes to the Turks had to be paid in silver and in time so great did this demand for silver become that a serious shortage of the metal developed, indeed, at a time when more silver was needed elsewhere for the economic needs of Europe, whose currencies were all based on the metal.

To try to offset this heavy drain on silver a thorough search was mounted in the second half of the fifteenth century for new sources of silver, as a result of which new mines were brought into operation in the Tyrol and in southern Bohemia. Of considerable benefit too was the devising about the same time of Bills of Exchange, whereby merchants were able to arrange for the future payment of their debts by signing papers, which stated the sums of money involved, naming a date and a place where the payment would take place. A centre of commerce and finance was always chosen, like Augsberg or Antwerp or Lyons, where merchants tended to foregather in numbers and where they were able to sort out their business problems. Useful as these Bills of Exchange turned out to be and equally useful as was the output of the new silver mines, European merchants searched for further ways to economise in the use of silver. If only, the entrepreneurs reasoned, new sea-routes could be found from eastern countries to Europe, which would be able to bypass the Turkish stranglehold on the caravan routes, the problem would be greatly eased. This thinking was to provide the impetus for daring voyages, whose effect was in time to change the course of history; by this time all navigators knew that the world was round but what they did not know was the size of the world, but, with the invaluable aid of the mariner's compass, which had recently come into general use, brave sailors set forth into uncharted seas. The wonderful era of the geographical discoveries was about to begin.

In 1486 the Portuguese navigator, Diaz found his way round the Cape of Good Hope into the Indian Ocean, to be followed up eleven years later by his fellow countryman Vasco da Gama, who succeeded in pioneering a voyage across the Indian Ocean to India; in between these two momentous voyages of discovery Christopher Columbus in 1492, financed and encouraged by Spain, sailed westwards across the Atlantic in an epic attempt to find a shorter route to the economic treasures of the East. Columbus, like all other contemporary navigators, had no knowledge of the existence of another continent to be encountered on a western voyage from Europe to Asia. When he stepped ashore in the New World, he probably thought that he was in Japan.

The upshot of these voyages and others that followed in the succeeding years was the establishment of trading companies, which set up trading posts along the new routes; their leaders soon came to realise the economic possibilities of the new situation or, to put it in modern economic terms, they visualised an enormous increase in raw materials and a possible outlet for the sale of goods, manufactured in Europe. In the seventeenth and eighteenth centuries English and French trading companies in particular took full advantage of the immense economic opportunities afforded; both countries were political rivals in Europe and at an approximately similar stage in their development as nation states. Their rivalry in Europe was accordingly widened and extended to America and India, where in time they took over from the existing trading companies, once the latter began to prove economically profitable. Peace treaties, signed at Utrecht in 1713 at the end of one war between them and again at Paris in 1763, at the end of another, rewarded the victorious English with greatly increased power and prestige in America and in India, thus laying the foundation of a considerable colonial empire.

The potential, implicit in the rapid increase in raw materials, could only be turned into reality, when proper use could be made of them, but the existing structure of industry in England was quite incapable of taking advantage of the chance, based as it was on the cottage system, whereby raw materials were delivered by middle men to workers' cottages, from which in due course the finished goods would be collected by them. Therefore in the early years of the eighteenth century there was a crying need for a conscious, deliberate search to be made for alternative methods of production; fortunately for the future of industrial production in England, though tragically for the welfare of the workers, man's ingenuity produced the steam engine, which, when applied to manual methods of production, gave rise to the factory system. The Industrial Revolution, by which is basically meant the application of steam to industrial processes, involved the building of factories to house the new steam-driven machinery and the erection on the same site of a great number of very small houses where the machine minders were to eke out their miserable existence.

By way of footnote to this chapter, some readers may like to know what happened to the spice trade, which had touched off the geographical discoveries, leading in their turn to the growth of colonial empires. In actual fact the need for spices soon began to dwindle, when farmers learned how to grow a winter feed for their cattle. The answer to their problem was provided by the turnip which was first grown in English gardens in the reign of Charles II; in the eighteenth century however its full potential as a winter feed was realised when Charles Townshend advocated its growth as a field crop. It was a most timely contribution to agricultural knowledge because not only did the autumn slaughter of cattle come to an end but the great increase in meat that in consequence became available made it possible later to feed the population which greatly increased in number as the new factory towns came into being.

History in Everyday Speech

Language is a living link with the past; every age enriches it with fresh allusions and references to contemporary events. Such accretions tend to be on trial for a generation or two before either falling out of favour or passing into general everyday use. To prove this point, two examples must suffice, both drawn from late Victorian England. The first one had to do with the brilliant career of one of the outstandingly successful soldiers of the day, who eventually became Field Marshal Viscount Garnet Wolseley. Born in 1833, he first saw active service in the Crimean War, participating in the siege of Sebastopol; thereafter he served with distinction in China, in India, on the Gold Coast and in Egypt. His name in the course of time became associated in the public mind with success, particularly as a result of what he achieved in the Ashanti campaign and in Egypt. His very name became a household word; for some years a common reply to a friend's enquiry as to "how are things with you?" would be "All Sir Garnet", indicating that everything was well, as indeed it had been for so many years in the distinguished soldier's career. "All Sir

Garnet" remained in use up to about fifty years ago, but it has hardly, if at all, been heard since 1945.

And yet the second example is still in general circulation, although it originated at about the same time. In 1886 Robert Cecil, the Marquis of Salisbury, became Prime Minister; in this, his second administration, he made a new appointment for the key position of Secretary of State for Ireland, nominating his own nephew, the young Member of Parliament, Arthur Balfour. It was a surprising choice which provoked some barbed comment, the general opinion, rightly or wrongly, being that it was by no means a political obstacle for a young politician to have a Prime Minister for an uncle! Thus, "Bob's your uncle" soon became common currency, but why "All Sir Garnet" died and "Bob's your uncle" lives remains an unsolved puzzle.

Sometimes in the course of the centuries, a word is changed without apparently the meaning of an aphorism connected with it being affected. The fourteenth century provides just such an illustration; this unhappy century of great change not only witnessed repeated outbreaks of plague but also suffered serious losses of sheep through disastrous epidemics of scab. Various remedies were tried, of which the most efficacious proved to be tar. Tar however was expensive but if it was to cure the disease, it had to be applied generously. The false economy practised by some farmers gave rise to the caveat "not to despoil good sheep for a hap'orth of tar", which later generations, becoming increasingly sware of Britain's growing prowess on the high seas, changed to "ship". A sobering picture was thus painted in the mind's eye of lazy sailors on board their black and white ships applying too little tar to the creaking timbers with predictably disastrous results! Today the warning is still given not to spoil the ship for a hap'orth of tar; to go back to the original would indeed be thought pedantic, though it is salutary to remember that we owe almost as much to our sheep as to our ships!

The Royal Navy has, however, furnished the language with a number of expressions, which have stood the test of time, even though the connection with nautical affairs is today anything but obvious. The three examples to be cited all stemmed from the Napoleonic Wars, which disturbed Europe for twenty long years, in which the Navy was constantly on active service. When, as occasionally had to happen, ships were in port in the United Kingdom, sailors were permitted to enjoy the company of their wives, who were allowed to live on board. However, naval discipline had to be maintained; hence it came about that when the bo'son went round in the morning to rouse the ship's company from their hammocks, he called out "Show a leg". Sailors and their wives both had to comply, but only those whose legs were free from hair were allowed to stay in the hammocks.

On several occasions during the war the fleet was based on Naples, where on one particular day shore leave was granted. A sailor, on his return to his ship in the evening, was asked where he had been and what he had seen. Not the most observant of men, he could only remember having seen a church. On being questioned further he admitted to having been inside and to have heard the congregation shout out "All my eye and Betty Martin". The reaction of his shipmates to this remarkable announcement has not been transmitted to posterity but the date of this shore leave is likely to have been November 11th, the feast of St Martin; it is probable that what the sailor actually heard was "Ah mihi, beate Martine", the beginning of the Latin invocation to St Martin!

Back in England, a year or two before the end of the same war, a maid servant, employed at a house in the Winchester district of Hampshire, disappeared, never to be found; elsewhere in the same county at about the same time the naval authorities in Portsmouth were conducting an experiment in preserving mutton for the use of the navy. Unfortunate sailors, who were made to act as guinea pigs, spurned the new food, pronouncing it to have a sweet and sickly taste, which caused them to link it with the missing maid servant, whose name was Fanny Adams! "Sweet Fanny Adams" started life then as naval slang, an expression which was originally used only to describe food that was unpleasant.

Napoleon Bonaparte was not the only menace that threatened

the peace in the eighteenth century; here at home law and order were frequently disturbed by robbers on the highway. There was as yet no one authority responsible for the upkeep of the roads, which in consequence were ill-maintained and by no means conducive to safe or comfortable travel. In addition, the coaches were still unwieldy and without benefit of springs; hence they often broke down to the considerable advantage of marauders on horseback. More often than not highwaymen escaped with their loot; the red-coated guards were armed only with slow and cumbersome blunderbusses. If, after a raid, highwaymen, as they rode off, heard a shot whistle past them, the normal comment that passed between them was "a miss is as good as a mile". In other words, the highwaymen expected to be a mile nearer complete safety before the guard would be able to reload his blunderbuss and fire a second shot.

The second half of the eighteenth century, which was to witness a great improvement in the state of the roads, also saw essential and important changes in agriculture. North of the border, the Duke of Argyll was in the vanguard of such reformers, his special contribution being in the realm of pig breeding. On his estate at Inverary Castle posts were driven into the ground at suitable intervals to enable his pampered pigs to scratch their backs and thus, it was hoped, subsequently to improve the quality of the bacon. Guests at the castle, it was reported, frequently availed themselves of these pig posts to alleviate their itching backs — facilities for taking a bath were not as good in the eighteenth century as they are now! The custom apparently grew up for the guests to mutter, as they scratched, "God bless the Duke of Argyll". The phrase passed into general usage when people scratched an itching back but it is rarely heard nowadays and is only understood by a small minority. In another few years it will join "All Sir Garnet" in oblivion.

In view of the central position occupied in English life throughout the middle ages by the parish church, it is perhaps surprising that so little reference to it remains in our language; one aphorism that has survived, however, relates to the nave, which was unconsecrated and to all intents and purposes the village meeting place. Here, where on weekdays both serious meetings and jovial parties took place, on Sundays parishoners were expected to assemble and to listen to the sermon but, as the only seats in the medieval nave were attached to the side walls and as the sermon was expected to last the full hour until the hour-glass above the pulpit was quite empty, only the strongest and the fittest could stay the course, it becoming necessary to help the faint-hearted through the ranks of the standing congregation to the welcoming walls, whence came the expression "the weak go to the wall".

An expression still in everyday use, which will soon be a hundred years old, was derived from the streets of London, at a time when they were still loud with the clatter of horses' hooves, the internal combustion engine not yet having displaced horses in public transport. Sometimes the drivers of these horse buses became to attached to their horses that they were known on their rest days to travel as fare-paying passengers on their own buses to make sure that their horses were being properly taken care of by their temporary drivers. Such generous men were said by their friends to be having a busman's holiday; their actions certainly deserve the posthumous fame which they still enjoy.

Of the many single words with interesting historical origins, one will here have to act as a stimulus to individual research — the word 'tawdry'. Behind tawdry there is a strange story. The word is a corruption of 'St Audrey', itself a corruption of Etheldreda, a seventh century Saxon princess, whose father was King of East Anglia. In 673 she withdrew from the world and founded a nunnery in the Isle of Ely. In the middle ages a fair was held every year on the saint's day, which was October 17th. At this St Audrey's Day fair the sale of silks and lace predominated but in the course of time standards deteriorated until the fair became associated with lace work of poor quality. Tawdry then, which was originally used only to describe the poor lace work at Ely Fair, passed gradually into the language to describe anything of a gaudy or trumpery nature.

Any reader anxious to follow up this line of research might with advantage start by looking up the origins of the cravat and the raglan coat, round robin, martinet and silhouette. As a postscript to this chapter, mention should perhaps be made of spiv, a word with a very modern connotation, which the dictionary defines as "a flashy black market hawker". In fact, spiv is already almost hallowed by age, since it started life nearly a hundred years ago as a nineteenth century Metropolitan police abbreviation for Suspected Persons and Itinerant Vagrants.

The Living Past in Wales

This chapter is unlike its predecessors, which dealt with a variety of topics, mainly concerned with aspects of social history. Here however the author, who is old and English, is about to indulge himself in writing about Wales, where some of the happiest and most rewarding hours of his life have been spent; in so doing he will be discharging an overdue debt of gratitude, which, he hopes, will induce others, on both sides of Offa's Dyke, to share his enthusiasm. There is more to this chapter however than the indulgence of one man's whim as Wales merits separate study because the pattern of her historical development differs so significantly from that of her eastern neighbour.

The Celts, the ancestors of Welshmen, arrived in Britain about 500 BC, whereas the forebears of a great many Englishmen came here a thousand years later, when the Saxons established themselves in eastern Britain. Early settlement patterns differed considerably but, after the withdrawal of the Roman legions at the beginning of the fifth century AD, darkness descended upon the land. Only a simpleton believes in the inevitability of progress, at best two steps forward being accompanied by one step backwards. The first great distinction between the Celtic way of life and the Saxon came in the course of the fifth century, when Christian missionaries arrived in south-west Wales from western parts of Gaul, probably from Brittany. Earlier Christian communities in Roman Britain had disappeared with the ebbing of Roman power, not to return until St Augustine landed in Kent in 597, nearly two centuries after successful Christian missions in many parts of Wales. Much archaeological evidence of this early Christian achievement in Wales in the fifth and early sixth centuries may be seen today not only in favoured museums such as those in Cardiff, Swansea, Margam, Carmarthen and Brecon but also in many a remote Welsh church, to which for safety's sake early Christian tombstones, inscribed in Latin, have been transferred from the surrounding churchyards.

Clynnog Fawr church

The past lives very vividly for me in many places in Wales, and although it is invidious to particularise, I have had to limit myself to making special mention of certain places, whose appeal is very special.

CLYNNOG FAWR. GR 414409.
Ten miles south-west of Caernarfon.

The very large cathedral-like parish church is dedicated to St Beuno, who in the seventh century moved westwards from his former home at Berriew, near Welshpool, and established a llan at Clynnog, which in time became a clas. After his death his grave there became a shrine which particularly attracted sick people, some of whom claimed miraculous cures there. In the previous century further west in the Llŷn Peninsula another early Christian missionary, St Cadfan had established a monastery on Bardsey Island, which before long became a focal point for would-be Christian missionaries. Their ranks were greatly swelled after the slaughter by the Saxons of 1500 monks at their monastery at Bangor Is-coed; the 900 survivors slowly made their way to Bardsey, one of their stopping places being Clynnog. Gradually thereafter a pilgrim's route crystallised, the main places that offered hospitality being Clynnog, Llanaelhaearn, Pistyll, Nefyn, Llangwnnadl and Aberdaron. In 1950 the ancient pilgrimage was revived; since then every August pilgrims have sallied forth from Clynnog en route for Bardsey, stopping at the traditional places.

There is much to see in Clynnog's great parish church; of special interest to many is a Celtic sundial, engraved on a free-standing pillar about six feet south of the south-west corner of St Beuno's Chapel. It is probably the second oldest churchyard sundial in Britain.

PISTYLL CHURCH. GR 328423

Follow the pilgrim route from Clynnog and four miles after passing through Llanaelhaearn but before reaching the village of Pistyll leave the B4417 and take a minor road on the seaward side which soon leads to St Beuno's church on the righthand side, on a mound above the road. Behind the church once lived the monks, who attended to the pilgrims' needs, their monastery now replaced by a working farm. The monks' fish-pond can be seen at the road-side.

Visitors who dare to peer over the steep slope south of the church will be able to identify a number of berried bushes, sloes, hawthorns, hops, blackberries and gooseberries, the descendants of bushes which long ago were tended by the monks and which, one hopes, provided sustenance for the pilgrims. In the flat churchyard will also be found medicinal herbs which will likewise owe their existence to medieval monks.

The interior of the church is a veritable time-warp; its

Pistyll church

rush-covered floor not only recalls former times but also draws our attention to the devoted friends of the church, who since the revival of the pilgrimage in 1950 have three times every year changed the rushes, at Easter, at Lammas and at Christmas, as well as decorating the church with shrubs and flowers that they gather from the churchyard.

LLANGELYNNIN CHURCH, CONWY VALLEY.
GR 752737

Nearly a thousand feet above the Conwy Valley and about two miles south-west of Henryd is St Celynnin's church. The approach is probably best made on foot, although a car may be taken up a narrow, unmade road and left near a farm, which is just below the church. The church today is remote and windswept and isolated, though in former times it served a thriving community in this bleak upland area and played an important part in the social life of the parish.

Llangelynnin

South of the church porch there are a number of table tombs, and there are signs elsewhere in the churchyard of a former cock-pit. The real reason for this visit is to see a remarkable well in the south corner of the churchyard, which is one of the very few surviving churchyard wells. It is in excellent condition, walled around (it used once to be roofed over) and there is seating accommodation both sides of the well. Over the centuries this well acquired a considerable reputation for curing the diseases of children; sick children were brought from a distance and lodged in local farms to enable them to get frequent access to the life-giving water.

GWYTHERIN, CONWY. GR 878617

At Gwytherin, a village high up under the Denbighshire moors, fact and fiction overlap; the church is dedicated to St Winifred, with whom a remarkable legend is concerned. Further east in Flint, the story goes, St Winifred lost her life in the 7th century, when she was decapitated in resisting a would-be rapist, a spring of

Gwytherin
— one of the stones in the Bronze Age alignment in the churchyard, being a Romano-British inscription.

water gushing up at the spot where her head struck the ground. Then it was, the story continues, that her famous uncle, St Beuno made a miraculous appearance and brought back to life his unfortunate niece by taking up her head and restoring it to her shoulders. Next he arranged for her to become the abbess of a convent at Gwytherin.

Her church in Gwytherin stands on a mound; the notion that this mound had been a Bronze Age site gained much credence by the alignment of four standing stones in the north side of the churchyard, each about three feet high and six feet apart. Enough has perhaps already been said to explain the appeal of Gwytherin to historically-minded enthusiasts, but there is more to follow. For, one of these standing stones bears a Latin inscription, commemorating one Vinnemaglus, the son of Senemaglus. Vinnemaglus is likely to have been an early Christian, who died in about the 6th century. Experts differ in their explanations, some claiming that the stones are of prehistoric origin, while other believe they all mark Christian burials. Another view is that the

Ysbyty Cynfyn
— a Bronze Age stone, within churchyard wall

inscribed stone dates from the Bronze Age, but was re-used many, many centuries later to mark the death of Vinnemaglus. It has to be added that of the many yew trees in the churchyard, two are over twenty-six feet in girth and have been expertly dated as being over two thousand years old.

YSBYTY CYNFYN Churchyard, CEREDIGION. GR 752791

Further evidence of an early Christian llan being set up on a site previously used in prehistoric times is furnished by the churchyard that surrounds the little church of Ysbyty Cynfyn, which lies twelve miles east of Aberystwyth, two miles north of Devil's Bridge, and twelve miles north of Strata Florida. The present church, an early Victorian building, the latest in a long line of churches, built on the original llan, stands in the middle of a churchyard, in whose stone wall are to be found five stones that belonged to a Bronze Age circle, of which three are probably still in their original position, while the other two have been re-sited to act as gateposts.

Pennant Melangell church, Llangynog, Powys
(Photo: Mick Sharp)

Ysbyty Cynfyn, whose first stone church is thought to have been built in the late twelfth century, acted from that time as a hospice, as its name implies, for travellers on their way to the Cistercian monastery, which was founded at Strata Florida in 1185.

PENNANT MELANGELL Church, POWYS. GR 024265

Hidden in the remote Pennant valley, west of Llangynog, at the foot of the Berwyn Mountains is the church of St Melangell, named after an eighth century Irish princess, who sought refuge in the valley to escape the unwanted attentions of a prince. Here one day another prince, Brochwel, of Powys, came hunting hares; one of the animals took refuge under the skirts of Melangell (*Monacella*). The prince, impressed by the refusal of the hounds to pursue their quarry and by the courage of Melangell, called off the chase, talked to Melangell and made her a grant of land in the valley, where she might build a nunnery, over which indeed she came to preside. Four centuries later a shrine in the Norman church, dedicated to her, was built to hold her earthly remains, which became a celebrated place of pilgrimage in the Middle Ages.

Today's pilgrims come to look at the depiction of the legend on the fifteenth century screen in the church, whose shrine of St Melangell was reconstructed in 1992. For a thousand years Pennant Melangell has been a place of pilgrimage; today it is not only a place for the historically-minded to come and marvel, it is also an oasis to which the sick, in mind and body, come for sanctuary.

In the eighteenth century Thomas Pennant visited Pennant Melangell; he wrote:

> "Till the last century so strong a superstition prevailed that no person would kill a hare in the parish; and even later when a hare was pursued by dogs, it was firmly believed that if anyone cried 'God and St Monacella be with you' it was sure to escape."

DISSERTH, POWYS. GR 034583

St Cewydd's peaceful church is to be found down a country cul-de-sac near the river Ithon, only two miles south-west of Llandrindod. The whitewashed church stands in the middle of a large nearly circular churchyard, whose north side is still free of graves. It is not difficult to call up the past here, as one passes under the ancient yews that guard the approach to the church. Once inside the building, time moves back to the seventeenth century, with all the box pews still in position, many of them still bearing the names of those who worshipped there, and all of them dominated by the triple-decker pulpit that rises above the nave.

Two hundred and fifty years ago a Shropshire lawyer chanced to pass that way on a July day when parishoners were busy celebrating their patronal day. He wrote it all down and his report, which happily survives, not only tells of dancing in the churchyard and the animated playing of games but also conjures up a memorable picture of a thriving parish in the long ago. Visitors who would like to share the lawyer's experience in 1744, are advised to consult the excellent church guide, which is available in the church.

Goats in Disserth churchyard

Partrishow

PARTRISHOW, POWYS. GR 279224

A pilgrim to Partrishow — and it is best to go there as a pilgrim — must first study the Ordnance Survey map and the Grid Reference. Immediately below the church at the foot of a short but steep hill is a well on the righthand side of the lane. Here the history of Partrishow began, for tradition has it that in the sixth century a Christian missionary, Issui settled in a hut near the well, where he conducted a most successful mission, healing the sick before converting them. Alas, one day he was murdered by a former patient whom he had cured. Thereafter his healing power was found to have been transferred to the well, which acquired much fame over the centuries for its many cures until in the eleventh century, the same tradition insists, a wealthy leper, cured at the well, in his gratitude paid for a church to be built at the top of the hill, which the Book of Llandaf says was erected in 1060.

Partrishow (*Patrisio* in Welsh) still stands alone in a churchyard, beyond whose ancient yews will be found a medieval preaching cross, complete with a calvary, tastefully added in the twentieth century. So remote was Partrishow in the past that the orders, given in London at the time of the Reformation to its commissioners to pull down the cross in the churchyard and to mutilate the consecration crosses, carved on the altars in the church, were never carried out as the church was never found. So today there are still six consecration crosses in the church and the marvellous preaching cross outside near the south door, from whose steps Archbishop Baldwin preached the Third Crusade in the twelfth century, and at his side his faithful chaplain, Giraldus Cambrensis. Perhaps the church is best known today for its quite wonderful fifteenth century screen, but the whole place, well, church and churchyard has an ambience all its own.

TRELECH, MONMOUTHSHIRE. GR 500054

Trelech, situated south of Monmouth, on the west side of the Wye, is today a large village which was once the county town. Its former importance is suggested by the size of the church, its antiquity by

Trelech

the presence in a field south of the houses of three standing stones, almost certainly belonging to the Bronze Age, which bear the anachronistic name of Harold's Stones! Saxon Harold, the last Saxon king of England, did indeed pass that way but about two thousand years after the erection of the stones, which give the place its name. In the church is a stone sundial, dated 1689, probably taken there for shelter, on whose base is depicted in stone the standing stones, accompanied by a Latin inscription, indicating that Saxon Harold gained the victory!

In a field east of the church is an ancient well, formerly known as St Anne's Well, known today as The Virtuous Well, which probably filled the first font in the parish church; indeed it may even, in the centuries before that, have supplied the needs of prehistoric man. The pride and joy of Trelech today is the outstanding churchyard cross, which very probably occupied the site where the first missionary there erected his simple wooden cross. Quite close to this cross is a "puzzle in stone"; it consists of a stone slab, about five feet long, and two feet wide. It is supported by low stone struts. In the absence of any firm knowledge it can be reasonably surmised that it belonged to Roman times, there having been in the area an as yet unexcavated Roman settlement.

The churchyard cross at Nevern.

NEVERN, PEMBROKESHIRE. GR 083401

Nevern lies halfway between Cardigan and Fishguard, and north-west of the Preseli hills. Early man settled here in Neolithic times, attracted by a bountiful supply of water in wells and streams. Evidence for this early settlement is provided by Pentre

Ifan, one of the finest Neolithic sites in Britain; it is about three miles south-west of Nevern.

Where the church now stands Brynach, an Irish missionary monk and a friend and contemporary of St David, set up a llan in the sixth century; proof of this is offered by two surviving Romano-British memorial stones, one inside the church, where it acts as a window sill, bearing an inscription to Maglicunus, both in Latin and in the Irish Ogham script, the other, outside the porch, where it marks the grave of Vitalianus, again in Latin and Ogham. Nevern would be famous for these two memorial stones alone, but in fact they are dwarfed in the public reckoning by the presence near the porch of a tenth century Celtic cross, thirteen feet high, and perfectly preserved. It is indeed one of the three great Celtic crosses of Wales, the others being at Carew, between Pembroke and Tenby, and at Whitford in Flint, Maen Achwynfan.

Nearby is an avenue of enormous yew trees, leading from the gate to the porch, with another twenty-six yews elsewhere in the churchyard. There is so much to see here, inside the church, in the churchyard and indeed near the church, including the Pilgrims' Cross, that it is hardly surprising that to many people Nevern is a very special place indeed.

LLANILLTUD FAWR, GLAMORGAN. GR 966687

Llanilltud Fawr (*Llantwit Major*), left to last because it is the most southerly place in the itinerary, is of outstanding interest and importance. For it was the birthplace of Christianity in Wales, as it was here that Illtud landed, when he sailed from Brittany at the end of the fifth century. Here, in today's large churchyard he planted his wooden cross and set up his llan as a prelude to preaching the Christian gospel. Illtud was a scholar, however, as well as a Christian missionary, and the llan became a clas and went on to become a college that produced not only Christian missionaries but also renowned scholars. In Illtud's lifetime this monastic college achieved as great a reputation for scholarship as it did for producing Christian missionaries. Among its early alumni were Cadog and Gildas.

Llantwit Major
(Llanilltud Fawr)

Today's visitors who want to sense the past would do well to enter the churchyard from the back, over a small bridge, whose water had enabled Illtud to set up his llan where he did. Today's very large and splendid church is a complicated structure because it is in reality two churches, joined by a central tower. The 'old' church, the western half of the building is Norman with later additions, while the 'new' part was built in the thirteenth century and is today's parish church. The 'old' part is now a museum, where there are a great many invaluable relics of the early Christian church, Christian crosses and memorial stones that over the years have been brought indoors from the churchyard for protection.

On this site Christianity has been preached for fifteen hundred years. Llanilltud Fawr is one of the glories of Wales.